TERI BARNETT

Pumpkins ARE MURDER

BIJOUX MYSTERY SERIES: BOOK 4

Pumpkins are Murder
Bijoux Mystery Series: Book 4
Published Internationally by Teri Barnett
USA

teribarnett.com
Lucky Crow Press

PRINT ISBN 978-1-7365413-4-0
EBOOK ISBN 978-1-7365413-5-7

Editor: Joanna D'Angelo

For Steve & Alice

ACKNOWLEDGMENTS

When I was invited to my first meeting in 1992, I had no idea what a huge part Indiana Writers' Workshop would play in my writing journey. Thank you for the encouragement, critiques, and community, with a special thank you to my beta reader, Jeff Stanger. And thank you, too, to Joanna D'Angelo, an amazing editor, great cheerleader, and dear friend.

CONTENTS

Chapter 1 1
Chapter 2 5
Chapter 3 9
Chapter 4 13
Chapter 5 19
Chapter 6 25
Chapter 7 31
Chapter 8 37
Chapter 9 43
Chapter 10 49
Chapter 11 55
Chapter 12 61
Chapter 13 67
Chapter 14 73
Chapter 15 79
Chapter 16 85
Chapter 17 91
Chapter 18 97
Chapter 19 105
Chapter 20 111
Chapter 21 121
Chapter 22 127
Chapter 23 133
Chapter 24 137
Chapter 25 145

Sneak Peek: Mistletoe is Murder 151
About the Author 155
Also by Teri Barnett 157

CHAPTER 1

"You are one ugly pumpkin," Ninja Jeff Malone whispered to the massive, odd-shaped gourd. The master pumpkin carver, who'd earned his nickname for his mad knife skills, was inspecting the crop of pumpkins in the middle of a field. "Nice and big but, beyond that, not at all what I'm looking for." He got down on all fours and foraged through the fog-covered vines, his movements stirring up an earthy smell. "My Spidey-senses tell me the perfect pumpkin is somewhere near here. I just know it is."

The sun was barely up, and the leaves glistened with dew. He'd purposely set out early so he could get a jump on the competition. This year's Pumpkins and Poe Festival was shaping up to be a tough one; all the big names in the biz were in attendance. Sitting back on his haunches he picked up Mr. Ugly again and gave it another once over. Weighing about fifty pounds, it certainly carried a lot of heft, but would it carry the day? Sometimes the ugliest pumpkins turned into the best jack-o-lanterns, depending on the skill and vision of the carver. "Although this one looks like it would be a definite challenge." His gaze strayed across the pumpkin hunting ground stretching out about two acres around him. "Finding the perfect pumpkin will be the key to winning that fifty grand."

"Hey!!! You!!!"

Startled by the shout, Jeff spun on his knees. The weight of the pumpkin caused him to lose his balance and he toppled sideways, hitting the ground hard, his head colliding with what felt like a sharp rock. He blinked a few times to try to clear his vision.

The hooded, black-cloaked figure crouched over him.

"Wha-What the hell?" Jeff sputtered. "Death? N-no way! N-not my time." He struggled to sit up.

The cloaked figure wagged a finger and shoved him back.

Jeff groaned as he fell back, his head smacking the rock again.

The figure glanced around and, pulling out a large pocket-knife, hacked at the thick vine attached to a large pumpkin.

"He-hey, Death, shouldn't you have a better knife than that?" Jeff muttered as he struggled to stay conscious.

Death shrugged as they held the pumpkin in their lap and stabbed the knife into the back of the gourd. Slicing out a large hole, they regarded Ninja Jeff's face. "You know it was convenient, you falling like that and banging your head," the voice rasped from beneath the black hood. "Not what I had originally planned, but all's well that ends well."

Jeff grunted as he tried to roll over and push himself up, but his arms gave out and he landed face down in the dirt. Blood trickled into his eyes from the gash on his head. He lay his hands flat on the ground and, with every ounce of strength he had, managed to roll onto his side. He reached out his hand. "Help me," he pleaded. "Please."

Death brushed a strand of blond hair away from Jeff's eyes and patted his cheek. "I'm sorry. Today's just not your day to win." The figure eased the pumpkin over Jeff's face and began to tug at the vines, pulling the surrounding pumpkins around and over the carver.

Jeff groaned; his voice muffled inside the pumpkin. His eyes blinking through the holes in the jack-o-lantern stared at Death as they tucked their knife back in their pocket and stood. With a final wave, Death turned and strode away.

Jeff screamed as loud as he could, but by now his voice was barely a broken whisper.

"You can fuss and posture all you like, Sinclaire. Nothing you say is going to convince me you're the better pumpkin carver."

Sinclaire Wild ran a hand through her long curly red hair and looked out over the pumpkin patch located just on the outskirts of Bijoux, Michigan. It was a cool fall morning, still early, but the sun was already bright, carrying the promise of dissipating the swirl of morning ground fog. She and Jimmy Stevens had decided to come an hour early to Gourds Galore and scope things out before the nine a.m. scheduled time for carvers to meet and select their pumpkins for Bijoux's Pumpkins and Poe Festival. She made her way down a row, looking side to side, Jimmy next her. "Why do you have to be such a jerk? I beat you fair and square at the New England Fall Festival."

"You jinxed me."

Sinclaire stopped and stared at her sometimes friend. Well, in truth, Jimmy Stevens was always her friend. They'd even dated for a while. Then the stress of competitive pumpkin carving, and her Siamese cat Hebrides, got between them. "I don't know how many times I have to say it, but I had nothing to do with your favorite knife breaking mid-carve." She harrumphed. "And you can't blame Hebrides for that, either." She lifted the fabric cat carrier slung over her shoulder and whispered to the feline, "Can he, Hebrides?"

Hebrides howled and Sinclaire grinned. "See? He had nothing to do with it."

Jimmy rolled his eyes and frowned. "Bobby Rumble says you're a gremlin."

"And why would you believe anything Bobby says? He just wants to get in your head, so you'll choke this weekend." Bobby Rumble was the self-proclaimed King of Carvers and had an ego the size of three pumpkin fields. With a bad boy attitude to match.

The pair started walking again. Jimmy looked at Sinclaire out of the corner of his eye. "For the record, I think you'd be a cute gremlin."

Sinclaire laughed and swatted him on the arm. A swatch of blue caught her eye. "Hey, what's that over there?" She pointed to a spot a few rows over. "See the blue color? Definitely not natural to pumpkins. Let's take a look." She carefully stepped over the vines, Jimmy following.

"This is really strange. Pumpkins and vines don't grow like this," Sinclaire commented as they approached the tangled mess. "I'm going to guess and say these have been purposely arranged. We should investigate."

Jimmy scoffed. "You watch too many true-crime shows." He leaned past her. "Looks like a scarecrow might have been knocked over. Most likely due to prankster kids or vengeful crows. Only logical explanation."

"You can believe in vengeful crows and that I'm a gremlin, but not that we should take a closer look? Well, I'm going to and if you want to help me shift some of these pumpkins then I would welcome the help. Otherwise, step aside." She squatted and moved a vine and a couple of smaller pumpkins carefully to the side so as not to damage them. "Definitely two denim covered shaped legs. Wait. Jimmy, is that blood on the pumpkin head? Around the bottom edge? And it looks like it's been freshly cut —that edge isn't dried out yet."

He looked over her shoulder and trained his cell phone flashlight where Sinclaire pointed. "Can't be. Pumpkins don't bleed. Neither do scarecrows. Here let me move some of these heavier ones." Jimmy pocketed his phone. He stepped around Sinclaire and bent to shift the large pumpkin. He screamed, stumbled backward, losing his grip on the gourd in the process.

Sinclaire gasped, "Holy Hecate! It's—it's Ninja Jeff!" She scrambled to her feet. "Jimmy, call 911!"

Jimmy whipped out his phone and dialed.

She began pulling at vines and shoving pumpkins away from the unmoving form. She leaned in. "He's not breathing!"

"What's your emergency?" the operator's voice said on speaker.

"I don't know how to explain this, but there's a ninja scarecrow here." Jimmy scrubbed a hand over his face, took a breath. "No. That's not right. Sorry. Not a scarecrow, just a ninja. A dead ninja. In the Gourds Galore pumpkin patch off M-22."

CHAPTER 2

"I HEREBY DECLARE my candidacy for mayor!"

Morgan Hart, captain, and half of the two-person police force in the lakeside tourist town of Bijoux, Michigan, population 5083, exchanged a confused glance with Deputy Jeremy 'JJ' Jones, the other half.

"Um, that's not how it works, Mr. Dominic," Morgan said to the seventy-five-year-old retired bank manager and full-time curmudgeon. "You have to file paperwork over at the clerk's office."

"Fiddle faddle. I know how to declare something," he insisted and thwacked his cane soundly on the polished oak top of the police station's front counter. The sound echoed against the light blue painted block walls.

"Hey. Careful with the counter," Morgan said. "I just had the top of that restored."

Mr. Dominic shot Morgan a narrow-eyed look, then hit his cane on the counter again, albeit a bit more gently this time. He grinned like a goblin for good measure.

"Seriously?"

"Forget them. C'mon, Auggie," Audrey Burns, Mr. Dominic's almost seventy-year-old girlfriend and recently retired pet lawyer, crooned as she tucked her arm through his. "If they won't help us, we'll take it to the streets. That's what we'll do!" She raised her fist in the air. "Power to the people!"

Mr. Dominic, who was all of five foot five, beamed as Audrey, standing at five foot seven, bent slightly to give him a kiss on his bald head. "I'm running for mayor!" he shouted as she escorted him out the front door. "I'm anti-line-cutting on Coffee Cake Day and Pro Fish any day! I love a good perch dinner!"

Caleb Joseph, owner of the Raven's Nest Bookstore, former gothic lit prof at U of M, best-selling romance writer, soon to be published mystery writer, and resident town hunk, wound past Mr. Dominic and Audrey, and strode into the police station. Setting a magenta box from Hannah's Heavenly Confections on the counter, he adjusted his black horned rim glasses and smiled at Morgan and JJ. "Good morning. What's up with Mr. D?"

Morgan pushed up from her chair. "He came here to declare he's running for mayor," she said, eyeing the box as she approached the counter.

"It looks like it's now a three-way race between you, Mr. Dominic, and Mayor Ed," JJ said, sitting on the corner of his desk.

"Oh my gosh. Pumpkin cupcakes! I've already had breakfast, but I'm pretty sure I can make room for one of these." Morgan marveled at the six delectable Halloween treats sitting in the box. She lifted one and inhaled its spicy sweet aroma. She slowly turned it left and right, admiring the rich orange buttercream frosting, evenly swirled over the cinnamon and nutmeg spiced cake, and dusted with just the right amount of glittery black bat sprinkles. She took a small nibble, making sure to include an equal distribution of icing and cake. Closing her eyes, she savored the blend of autumnal flavors. "Perfection."

Cal cleared his throat. "JJ? You want one?"

JJ straightened and took two steps, stopped, turned, and plunked himself down on his chair. "Can't. Haven't been able to look a cupcake in the eye since Hannah broke up with me." He hung his head and ran his hands through his short red hair.

Cal reached into his brown corduroy jacket pocket, pulled out a waxed paper bag, and held it up, swinging it back and forth. "You know I have your back. How does a honey cruller from Dave's Deli sound instead?"

JJ's eyes widened and he rushed up to the counter. Snatching up the bag, he took a big bite of the donut and let out a groan. "I take back all the bad things I've ever said about you, buddy." He swallowed, took another bite, and talked around it. "Well, most of them."

"What is it with you two and baked goods?" Cal chuckled.

"Police business," Morgan said, smiling. "So, have you also officially declared your run for mayor in some weird and random way?

Like Mr. Dominic?" she asked Cal. She picked off a tiny shiny bat and popped it into her mouth.

"Nothing as dramatic as Mr. D. I did what normal people do and filed with the town clerk last week and, with the election only a few days away, I need to get busy letting more people know I'm running. Well, beyond the notices I've put up over at the shop. I'm thinking I should get some posterboard and markers and make some signs to hang up around town."

Morgan snorted. "What are you? Eight years old? Get some real signs. The printer in Grand Pere does great rush jobs. Dad just used them for some Halloween sale flyers for the store." Morgan's dad, Able Hart, had retired after thirty years as police captain and, along with Morgan's psychic stepmom, Zoe Buffet, now owned Hal's Hardware, the unofficial gathering place in Bijoux and purveyor of deliciousness on Coffee Cake Day.

"Good idea," Cal said. "I'll head over there after my meeting with Tess Clooney at the town hall. She's the new coordinator and wants to go over some last-minute details about this weekend's Pumpkins and Poe Festival."

"How is that going for you? I know how much you like running the town events and weren't happy turning over the reins of the festival to the town council," Morgan said.

"They think they can do better; I say let them." Cal shrugged and straightened his jacket. "I'm over it."

Morgan suppressed a smile. She'd learned early on that Cal's habit of pulling on his jacket was one of his 'tells.' "At least if you're not in charge, maybe no one will get murdered this time around," she offered.

Cal rolled his eyes. "We all know the murders weren't my fault." He paused. "Maybe I should run on that platform. No New Murders. Yes, that's it. I'm the Anti-Murder candidate."

The phone rang and JJ answered. "Bijoux Police...What? Are they sure?" He stood and started pacing while he talked. "Yeah, yeah. Okay. We'll be right there." He hung up the call. "You might want to hold that thought, Cal."

"No," Morgan said around a mouthful of cupcake. "You have got to be kidding me."

"I wish it *was* a joke." JJ sighed and grabbed his coat. "We have what appears to be a male body out at Gourds Galore. Whoever called it in must've been in shock because they're insisting it's some sort of ninja. Found under a pile of pumpkins and vines." His eyes met Morgan's and Cal's. "Normally, I'd think it was the local kids messing around with the scarecrows out there. Want to wait and call Doc McVie until after we check it out?"

"Yeah, let's take a look first." Morgan shrugged on her jacket. "But after the year we've had so far, anything is possible. Even a dead ninja."

CHAPTER 3

MORGAN AND JJ climbed into the department's blue Ford Ranger and waved at a disappointed Cal, who had to leave for his festival meeting with Tess.

"Feels weird to not have him tagging along," JJ said.

"What it feels like is normal." Morgan shot Cal a look in the rearview mirror as she pulled away from the curb. He turned and walked toward Bijoux's small town hall next door. If she were being completely honest with herself, it did feel a little strange not to have him crammed into the small truck cab with them. She glanced over at JJ. "Did he sign the indemnification paperwork, so we're covered if anything happens to him?"

"That he did. I scanned it in and it's in the new Caleb Joseph file I set up on the hard drive and the cloud."

Morgan chuckled. "I'm sure he'll appreciate knowing he now has an official file with the police. He'll probably think it makes him cool or rakish or something."

"That does sound like the professor," JJ said, laughing.

She turned the truck off Main Street, down an alley shortcut, and onto Highway M-22 and headed north. The end of October saw the birch trees wearing deep golden yellow leaves, in stark contrast to the evergreen forests they were interspersed with. Lake Michigan, to her left, was dark and choppy today, despite the clear skies. Another sign of the coming winter.

"The pumpkin patch is just ahead, on the right," JJ said.

"Thanks, I remember." Morgan smiled. "Mom and Dad used to bring me here when I was a kid. The apple cider and cake donuts were the best, as was the hayride to pick out your pumpkin."

"It was the place to be in October, that's for sure," JJ said. "Still is."

"If memory serves me correctly, the patch was owned and farmed by an older couple. Are they still around?"

"That would be the Rowans. Jesse died a few years back, but Opal is still going strong, even though she's in her eighties now. She has a group of high school kids she pays to help her plant and keep things going every season."

"Okay, let's keep that in mind. Depending on what we find, we may want a list of the teenagers for interviews."

Morgan slowed and pulled the truck onto the gravel road leading to Gourds Galore. The place was just as she remembered: a large red barn off to the left, a run-down farmhouse with a wraparound porch near the end of the drive, and pumpkins as far as the eye could see ahead and to the right. The barn door was ajar, revealing the old hay wagon. The memory of fresh hay and kids laughing popped into Morgan's brain and she smiled. She turned into a gravel lot and parked next to an orange SUV. Two people were huddled together near the other vehicle. She and JJ exited the truck and approached the pair. "I'm Captain Morgan Hart. This is Deputy JJ Jones. Were you the ones who found the body?"

The woman, slight build, maybe mid-twenties with a face full of freckles and curly red hair past her shoulders, nodded. "I'm Sinclaire Wild. This is Jimmy Stevens."

Morgan looked at the man. About the same age, taller and lean, shaggy brown hair like he was overdue for a haircut.

"Yeah, we found the ninja," Jimmy said, his voice shaky and eyes wide.

"A ninja?" JJ asked. He'd pulled a small tablet from his pocket and was tapping in notes. "Why do you think it's a ninja?"

"Not 'a' ninja. *The* ninja," Sinclaire corrected. "He's over here." She turned and started down one of the rows. Morgan, JJ, and Jimmy followed behind. Sinclaire stopped just past the body.

Morgan pulled on a pair of nitrile gloves and JJ started taking photos with his tablet. She squatted down and checked for a pulse. None. She looked at JJ and shook her head.

JJ pulled out his phone and made the call. "Doc will be here in twenty."

"Thanks." Morgan leaned back and surveyed the scene before her —a man, late twenties-early thirties, lay on his back, head turned. The only blood she could see was on the back of his head and the half-buried rock next to him, indicating he likely fell and hit it when he landed. But she'd leave that to Doc to decide. She stood and looked at Sinclaire and Jimmy. "You know the victim? You called him a ninja."

"That's Ninja Jeff. He's one of the best pumpkin carvers around," Sinclaire said. "He's in town for the Pumpkins and Poe carving competition." She glanced at Jimmy. "Just like us."

"Does Ninja Jeff have a last name?" Morgan asked.

"Yeah. Malone. I think he's from Illinois," Jimmy answered. He rubbed the back of his neck. "But I'm not sure."

"This area is highly disturbed. Did you two do this?" JJ asked, pointing at the space around Jeff. The vines were pulled and twisted, and small pumpkins were scattered on either side of the body.

"Um, well, yes and no," Sinclaire said. "We were here early to look at the pumpkins ahead of the picking event. I spotted a scrap of blue over here, thought it was strange, so we checked it out." She gestured to the body. "Now I know it's his pants. But I didn't know then—not like it's a color natural to the surroundings. The vines and pumpkins had already been moved around, covering him. I pulled them back and, well, we found Jeff." She shivered and pulled her black sweater tighter around her body. "I can't believe in a million years he fell, hit his head, and then decided to cover himself up like that. I'm calling it a murder."

Morgan raised an eyebrow. "How about you leave that part to us?"

Jimmy pointed a thumb at Sinclaire. "She thinks she's a detective. Watches way too many true crime shows."

"I have an eye for detail." Sinclaire scowled at her friend. "It's why I beat you at pumpkin carving," she added with a finger jab to his arm. Her cat let out a long growl. "See? Even he agrees with me." Sinclaire lifted the cat carrier from her shoulder and peered inside at the feline.

"What's with the cat?" Morgan asked, making a mental note to look into one of those carriers for Griselda. Maybe there was one she could fasten to the pillion seat on her vintage Triumph Bonneville motorcycle. The black Maine Coon was the type of cat who might like the feel of wind in her fur.

"This is my best friend, Hebrides. He goes everywhere with me. And he does not agree with Jimmy here." She lowered her voice to a whisper. "He senses something is off."

Everyone glanced around the field, then looked back down at Ninja Jeff.

"WHAT DO you have for me this bright and beautiful autumn morning?" Doc Fleetwood McVie, Bijoux's medical examiner, mortician, and family practice doctor—whose parents named him after their favorite band of all time, Fleetwood Mac—asked as he approached the crime site. "Did I hear something about a ninja?" He stopped, adjusted his wire rimmed glasses, and looked down at the body. "He's wearing jeans and a brown flannel shirt. I thought ninjas wore all black." He pulled on a pair of nitrile gloves and squatted down. "More of a scarecrow look, don't you think?"

"Exactly what I was thinking," JJ said.

"Ninja is apparently his nickname," Morgan added. She watched as Doc did his thing—checking body temp and briefly examining the head wound. He gently rolled Jeff onto his back. "Wait. What's that?" She squatted down and pointed at a piece of paper. JJ took a pic, then she held it up and read the note, scrawled in orange ink. One word. "Nevermore."

CHAPTER 1

MORGAN STOOD about ten feet away from Ninja Jeff, surveying the scene, and motioned for Doc McVie to join her. JJ followed, leaving Sinclaire and Jimmy still standing near the body with an admonishment not to touch anything. "What do you think? Is this just a random accident, or something else?" she asked.

Doc shrugged. "It looks like an accident. Except—"

"Except what?" JJ asked.

"Except there are two wounds on his head. There's a lot of blood, so it's hard to see any exact patterning. And the pumpkin innards all over his face make me wonder."

"What are you thinking, Doc?" Morgan asked.

He shook his head. "I'm ruminating here, imagining what might have happened to this poor man, which has no bearing either way on the truth, so I'll stop. I'll know more once I get him cleaned up and examined."

"Maybe he got up, was dizzy, and fell back down?" Morgan offered. "But there is the witness statement he was covered with vines and pumpkins when they found him, including one pumpkin lodged over his face. And that strange note."

Doc shrugged again. "Like I said. No more guessing. I won't know more until I can look more closely at him."

"All right." Morgan patted Doc's arm. "Thanks for your help. Please let me know as soon as you can."

"I always do." Doc nodded. "If you'll excuse me, I'll get him prepped for transport."

"Thanks, Doc." Morgan nodded at Doc and then approached the duo who'd discovered the body. "Sinclaire? Jimmy? You're free to go for now but please stay in town in case we have more questions."

Sinclaire leaned in and stage-whispered, "So you *do* think this is a murder?"

"That's not what I said."

"But you have to admit this is all a little suspicious."

Morgan sighed. She'd seen this before, back in Detroit and right here in Bijoux, with Cal. Amateur detectives trying to solve cases. And she knew from experience it would do no good to try to deter the younger woman. If anything, it would probably make her try to get even more involved. "If you hear anything, either of you," she nodded at Jimmy who was standing near Sinclaire, "please let either JJ or myself know. Okay?"

"We can do that. You can count on us." Sinclaire pointed to a group of people on the other side of the pumpkin patch. "Jimmy, they're getting ready to pick pumpkins." She looked at Morgan. "It's time to select our big orange canvases for this weekend's carving competition."

Morgan looked at JJ, frowning, as the pair left.

He pulled a roll of bright yellow caution tape out of his backpack and held it up. "Already on it. I'll cordon the area off, then let the group over there know to stay away from this area."

"Hey! JJ!" Connie Graham, local news reporter and Morgan's nemesis since childhood, shouted from where she stood at the edge of the parking lot. "What can you tell me about the crime scene?"

"Shouldn't you be talking to the captain?" He glanced over his shoulder and nodded behind him while he worked. "She's right there."

"Go away, Connie," Morgan said as she and Doc walked up to the lot. "I have nothing for you."

"You never do. And that's exactly why I'm talking to your deputy." She glanced furtively at Doc and gave him a little finger wave. "Oh. Hi, Woodsy."

Doc shook his head and kept walking. Morgan noticed his assistant, Maggie Cornet, who had a big crush on JJ, had arrived and was waiting by the town ambulance. Or hearse, depending on what it was needed for. "C'mon, Maggie. We have a body to load." The pair pulled the wheeled cart out of the back of the wagon, along with a body bag, and rolled it down the dirt path.

"I thought you and Wood were back together," Morgan said to Connie. Doc and Connie had been on the outs lately due to her snooping whenever he got a call and then showing up at Morgan's crime scenes.

"It's undecided at this point," Connie said. "But I have hope. And no, he didn't tell me about this." She gestured toward the field. "I overheard Cal telling Tess that you and JJ were out here with a possible dead scarecrow. Sounded interesting so thought I'd check it out." Connie tapped the record button on her phone. "I'm here at Gourds Galore with Captain Morgan Hart. Captain Hart, what can you tell me about the body discovered in the pumpkin patch this morning? Is it an unfortunate accident?" She held her phone in front of Morgan's face. "Or has there been another murder in our quaint little lakeside town?"

Morgan pushed Connie's hand aside. "Nothing to tell right now, Connie. You know I have to wait for Doc's assessment." She started walking toward the truck.

Connie frowned, then said into her phone, "It would seem the captain is surlier than usual. I can only attribute it to the fact she's obviously missing her frequent sidekick, Caleb Joseph, owner of the Raven's Nest Bookstore."

Morgan stopped. *What the hell?* She spun around. "I've heard you say some crazy stuff over the years, Connie, but that was absolutely one of the most ridiculous."

"Oh, please, the entire town has been privy to your whole 'will they or won't they' drama." She said the last part with air quotes and all but sneered at Morgan. "It's been playing out pretty much since you came back to Bijoux. And I notice you're not denying it."

"I will not comment on my personal life. It is completely off limits to you and your news reporting." Morgan stared hard at the other woman. "Understood?"

"Whatever you say, Morgan." Connie shut off the recording. "Whatever you say."

"Connie, do you know why caution tape is yellow?" JJ asked from behind Connie. She turned around.

"I have no idea, actually."

JJ pulled a new roll out of his backpack and held it out. Connie took it and turned the roll over in her hand. He stepped away from Morgan. "Come on over here and I'll explain the psychology of the color yellow and its association with caution tape. Maybe it'll give you a filler for your story since we don't have any facts about this case yet."

"Good idea." She smiled. "Thank you."

Morgan also smiled and mouthed an *I owe you* to her deputy, then walked toward the farmhouse. An old woman, dressed in purple, her silver hair plaited in a braid down her back, was sitting on the large, weathered wraparound porch, rocking, and sipping tea. "Opal?"

Opal nodded and pointed to the chair next to her. "Sit."

Morgan suppressed a smile. "Yes, ma'am. I'm Captain Morgan Hart and I'd like to ask you a few questions, if you don't mind."

"I know who you are. I don't forget anybody. You used to come here with your mom and dad." She paused, as if searching her memory. "Able and Billie. That one over there used to come with you, too." Opal pointed at Connie. "Doesn't seem like you two stayed friends, though."

"That would be an understatement. How do you remember all of that?"

Opal smiled and the corners of her mouth disappeared into the lines on her face. "Good herbs. Plus, some specific crystals and stones I keep on the nightstand next to my bed. They keep me sharp."

It was like talking to her stepmom, Zoe Buffett, Morgan thought. "Good to know. So, did you see anything earlier this morning? Out in the field over there?" Morgan motioned with her head toward the taped off area.

Opal stopped rocking. "I did. I saw a man, blond hair, in a brown flannel shirt. He was walking down the rows, talking to himself. Or maybe he was talking to the pumpkins. People do that sometimes, you know. It was hard to tell from this distance." She tapped her chin. "And someone in a black robe was walking the fields, too."

"Does that happen often? People walking through your pumpkin patch?"

"Not unusual this time of year." She started rocking again.

"The dead man fits your description. Can you tell me anything about the other person? Like their body size? Male or female?"

"They were wearing a loose robe, so no way of knowing the size." Opal sipped something from her ancient teacup. "Also, didn't say it was a person."

"Well, what else would it be?"

The old woman shrugged. "Specter. Ghost. Witch. I get all kinds out here."

"All kinds of people dressed up like those things, you mean." Morgan looked out over the pumpkin patch. The sun was bright against a deep blue sky and the ground fog had dissipated.

Another sip, more rocking. "If you say so."

Okay. Definitely like talking to Zoe. "Anything that might distinguish this particular *being* from any others wandering about? Perhaps a limp or something like that?"

"Now that you mention it—"

Morgan leaned in. "Yes?"

Opal thought for a moment longer, then shook her head. "Nope. Got nothing."

Morgan sighed. "Okay. If you think of anything, no matter how minor it might seem, would you please give me a call?" Morgan stood, pulled a card from her shirt pocket, and handed it to the other woman.

"Oh, I expect we'll be talking soon," Opal said with a twinkle in her eye.

Morgan started to say something, then closed her mouth. Instead, she just waved at Opal as she left.

CHAPTER 5

"MORGAN! MORGAN HART!"

Morgan turned just as she started to climb into the truck. Tess Clooney, Bijoux's recently hired town coordinator, mid-thirty something with a shoulder length brunette bob and pristine overalls, was heading her way.

"We haven't officially met yet." Tess extended her hand. "Tess Clooney. It's nice to finally meet the famous Captain Morgan." Tess giggled. "Well, the *other* famous Captain Morgan."

Morgan gave a sigh of exasperation as she shook the other woman's hand. "Is there something I can help you with?"

Tess pulled a piece of paper out of her back pocket and handed it to Morgan. "Cal said you might want this."

Morgan unfolded the paper. "Is this a list of all the carvers participating in the event this weekend?"

"It is." Tess nodded. "You don't seem too happy, though. Was it a mistake to give you that?" She lowered her voice to a whisper. "Was Cal wrong?"

"Just a lot on my mind at the moment, as I'm sure you can imagine. Also, no need to whisper about it, Cal is often wrong," Morgan said with a smile. "I planned on asking you for this, so thank you for being proactive." She slipped the paper in the truck's driver's side sun visor. "Have you heard any chatter about Jeff Malone from any of the other pumpkin carvers?"

"No, not really. I mean, some of them are visibly upset. I'm learning from being around them this morning it's a highly competitive field. Ninja Jeff was one of the better carvers, so no one's complaining at this point about him being gone."

"Harsh," JJ said as he walked up.

Tess nodded. "Definitely."

Morgan looked from JJ to Tess. "Well then. Please let me know if you hear anything." She handed Tess one of her business cards. "And thank you for the list."

"Ms. Clooney!" One of the carvers shouted from the field. "Are we allowed to look over here?" He pointed to an area just north of where Sinclaire and Jimmy had found Ninja Jeff.

Tess glanced at Morgan, who shook her head. "Nope. Stay away from the taped area, okay?"

"Of course," Tess said. "No! Stay over that direction!" she shouted back, waving her arm to the west. "Oh, I really should go and wrangle them."

"I'll let you know if I have any questions. Thank you again," Morgan said as she sat in the truck and closed the door. She rolled down the window. "You need anything else from me?" she asked JJ.

"Nope. I'm good here. I found some footprints under the vines, but they didn't lead anywhere. Also, some random fibers. I've bagged those and I'm going to take some measurements and photos of the prints." JJ glanced at his wristwatch. "I'll get a ride back to town with Doc, see if I can get him to hit a drive-thru. You want anything?"

"Thanks, but I'm going to grab a bite on my way back. I had an English muffin for breakfast, and that cupcake Cal brought over, but none of it's sticking." Her stomach growled as if confirming her statement and she clapped her hand over it. "See you in a bit."

JJ saluted as Morgan drove off. She glanced in her rearview mirror. Tess was heading back across the field toward the group of participants, where several seemed to be arguing over a particularly large pumpkin. She refocused on the road and shook her head. "Better her than me."

"WHAT WILL you have this unseasonably warm fall day?" Jerome, the ever-opinionated waiter at Dave's Deli, asked Morgan as she sat in her usual booth near the window. Sitting here gave her a vantage point to people watch and keep an eye on this part of town.

Morgan started to answer when Jerome held up his hand. "Wait. Let me guess. Burger, fries, diet Coke. Am I right?"

"Am I that predictable?"

Jerome shrugged. "You usually get that or a grilled cheese. I figured I had a fifty-fifty shot."

"Burger, please. But iced tea instead of pop."

"I'll have the same," Cal said as he slid into the booth seat opposite Morgan. "No. Wait. Scratch that. Cobb salad and unsweetened iced tea. And I'll take it to go." He patted his stomach. "I need to get ahead of all the treats I'm planning on eating during the Pumpkins and Poe festival."

"Slow day at the bookstore?" Morgan asked. "I'd think you'd be busy with all the visitors in town this weekend."

"That I am, swamped even, but Zoe came in to pick up a book order and offered to watch things while I grabbed some food." He rested his arms on the blue Formica table. "So, what can you tell me about our case?"

"Cal—"

"Morgan—" He waggled his eyebrows up and down.

"Dammit. I don't know why I have to keep telling you this. This is not *our* case. None of the cases have been *ours*." Morgan leaned back against the red vinyl seat and blew a strand of hair out of her eyes. "You make me tired; you know that?"

"I figure at some point you'll stop fighting me and acquiesce to the reality that I'm here and I'm helping. After I'm elected mayor, you may even see more of me."

"Assuming you do get elected. Did you get those signs ordered?"

"That I did. They'll be ready by the end of day. I have Billy Livernois coming over to watch the shop for the last hour and close up for me so I can head over to Grand Pere to pick them up."

"That's a lot of responsibility for him." Billy was one of the local high school kids, a senior this year, who had a bad habit of tagging murals and signs with giant porn star type mustaches. "How is he doing?"

"He's doing great, just needed some direction and focus. He's actually been working on college applications. Sent his first one into Michigan State yesterday from the shop."

"Michigan State?" Morgan laughed. "That must make you a little crazy."

Cal held up his hands. "Kids these days. What are you going to do? On the flip side, he's also applying to U of M, so he may become a Wolverine yet."

Jerome placed Morgan's plate of food and drink and Cal's to go order on the table. "Enjoy," he said and walked away.

"Huh," Morgan said.

"What?"

"It's Jerome. Is it me, or is he subdued of late? I mean, he didn't even comment on my food choices. You know he always has something to say about how unhealthy he thinks I eat."

Cal tapped the side of his head. "Maybe he doesn't have to anymore because he knows he's in your head now."

Morgan squirted some ketchup on her plate and dragged a couple of fries through it before popping them in her mouth. "Diabolical."

"Indeed." Cal popped the lid off the Styrofoam cup of iced tea and sprinkled in some raw sugar. "So, about that body this morning—"

"Fine. I'll tell you." Morgan sighed. "But only because it helps me to sometimes talk through what I'm thinking. *Not* because you're helping." She took a bite of her burger and swallowed. "Turns out it really was a ninja. Well, that was his nickname. Ninja Jeff. One of the pumpkin carvers in town for the competition this weekend. A couple of the other carvers found him wrapped in vines with a pumpkin shoved over his face. They're the ones who called it in."

"A-hah!" Cal slapped his hand down on the table. "I knew it!"

Morgan leaned back and eyed him warily. "Not the reaction I expected."

"Don't you see? This proves I'm not the catalyst or the albatross or whatever. This murder happened *after* the town took the event away from me."

"Oh, please with all the drama." Morgan sighed and ate another fry. "I didn't say it was a murder."

"You didn't have to. I know you, Morgan. You're only ever willing to talk things through when you're trying to put the puzzle pieces together on a murder investigation."

"*You* were the one who asked me what was going on."

Cal scooped up his bagged lunch and tea and slid out of the booth. He looked down at Morgan, grinning. "What I know is I'm feeling vindicated."

"Are you now? Then how about you tell me where you were early this morning? Before you came to the police station?"

Cal's grin faded. "What are you saying?"

"Maybe you wanted to pay the town back for removing you as event coordinator...show them up." Morgan knew Cal would never kill anyone unless it was self-defense, but his cocky and self-righteous attitude was annoying as heck. Besides, the confused/irritated look on his face made it oh so worth it.

"You're not serious." Cal stared at her, his mouth in a tight straight line.

Morgan shrugged. "Maybe. Maybe not. I'm waiting for Doc to give me his testing and autopsy results, then we'll see."

Cal tilted his head and relaxed back into his seat. His eyes narrowed slightly as he continued to stare at her. Morgan felt her stomach flip, so she took another bite of her hamburger.

"I get it. You have a need to act out since you know full well I was never a catalyst for any of the previous murders. It was just plain coincidence."

"Stop making me sound like a three-year-old. Questioning you after your overly happy reaction to the murder was legitimate and you know it."

"You might think you can rile me, but I've been watching you for a while now, Captain." He tapped his head and winked at her. "Just like Jerome, I'm in your head now, too."

CHAPTER C

"HAVE we heard anything from Doc yet?" Morgan asked JJ as she walked into the police station. It was midafternoon and Doc McVie was usually pretty quick with providing his initial assessments.

JJ glanced up from his computer. "Not yet. I've been working on identifying the shoe tread from the footprint I found, but the ground was too soft from the humidity this morning. Made getting a clean image near impossible."

Morgan perched on the edge of her desk and picked up her mini–Bubbles Power Puff Girls action figure. She tossed it up and down. "I've been thinking."

JJ swiveled chair to face her. "That it's time to retire the Girls?"

"What? No! Why would I do that?" She scowled.

He held up his hands. "Sorry! I'll go with the obvious then. You're wondering whether we have an accident or a murder on our hands?"

"Exactly. The way I see it, it's going to depend on if landing on the rock was enough to kill Jeff or if it was something else."

"But he was covered with pumpkins and vines, with one pumpkin over his face. At least according to our witnesses."

"We know people do strange things. Maybe someone found Jeff, he was already dead, and they covered him up so as not to interfere with the competition." Morgan shrugged. "Possibly thinking a dead body might put a stop to things."

"That would definitely be evil. And illegal, tampering with a body like that."

"Speaking of evil, when I talked to Opal earlier, she mentioned seeing a black robed figure walking across the field about the same time Jeff was out there. She thought they might have been together."

"And that didn't seem weird to her?"

Morgan shook her head and laughed a little. "Apparently not. She's insisting it wasn't human. The options she gave me were all supernatural beings."

The station door opened, and JJ and Morgan looked over. "Hi guys. JJ, can you give me a hand?" Doc's assistant, Maggie, was standing wedged between the door and frame and balancing two cardboard file boxes.

JJ jumped up and grabbed the door, pulling it open. Maggie smiled her thanks as she placed the boxes on the counter. "This is everything the deceased was either wearing or had on their person." She lifted the top of one of the boxes, pulled out a folder, and placed it on the counter. "And here is Doc's report."

Morgan picked up it. "Thanks for bringing everything over, Maggie. Much appreciated."

"Oh, no trouble at all." Maggie rested her elbows on the counter. "So, JJ, want to grab some dinner tomorrow night?"

Morgan looked from Maggie to JJ. Maggie and JJ had dated a few years back and it was no secret she still had a huge crush on the deputy. Now that JJ and Hannah were on the outs, Maggie was obviously making another move. "I'll just go read this in the back," Morgan said, holding up the folder. "Give you two some space."

"No!" JJ said a little too forcefully. "I mean, space is not needed." He looked at Maggie. "Thank you. But no."

Maggie frowned. "I thought we were friends, JJ. Can't two friends get a meal together? I was thinking of hitting some of the food trucks in town and checking out some of the Halloween festivities." She shrugged. "But if you can't even be friends with me, I guess I'll leave you alone from now on."

He let out a long sigh. "Okay, okay. We can hang out *as friends* and as long as the captain here doesn't need me on the case."

Maggie smiled and Morgan noted it was a little too triumphant.

"Call me," Maggie said as she exited the station.

"Really?" Morgan asked JJ.

JJ slumped in his chair. "She finally wore me down. It's probably the lack of sugar in my system. Low blood sugar can cloud your thinking." He rested his head on his desk and mumbled, "I miss Hannah."

Morgan sat on the corner of her desk. "I really am sorry, JJ. But I still have faith you two will figure it out." She opened the file and scanned the summary page. "Would it cheer you up to know we have a case?"

JJ raised his head and sniffed. "Maybe."

"Well, Doc says the two wounds on the back of the victim's head had patterning consistent with hitting the bloody rock we saw near the body. But he also discovered fibrous strands and seeds—what I'd call pumpkin innards—in the victim's nose, mouth, and throat." Morgan started pacing while she read. "He also says even though the head wounds would have been an issue, they weren't life threatening. Cause of death is asphyxiation." She stopped and looked at JJ. "By pumpkin."

"Well, that's a new one. I don't recall Doc giving us time of death at the scene. Does he say anything in the report?"

"About ninety minutes before we got the call." Morgan blew out a breath. "I'll state the obvious—Jeff did not put that pumpkin over his own face. We have another murder on our hands." She pulled the list of carvers from her shirt pocket and handed it to JJ. "Tess gave me this when we were at Gourds Galore. Could you start running checks on the remaining seven participants? Let's start with Sinclaire and Jimmy, since they found the body."

JJ took the list and looked it over. "Do you suspect either of them?"

"No, not really, but we still need to check. I'm going to head to the town hall and let Mayor Ed know what's going on. I saw him going in when I pulled up to the station."

"He is not going to be happy about this. We're just days away from the election."

Morgan rolled her eyes. "Which always seems to be more important to him than anything else."

"Kind of makes me hope Cal wins. He'd at least be more compassionate about people getting killed."

"You'd think, wouldn't you? He dropped in when I was at Dave's and asked about the case. Of course, I didn't say it was a murder because we didn't know for certain." Morgan shook her head. "Nevertheless, he cackled like a hen. Vindication, he called it."

"The professor doesn't like to show it, but he really was upset over Ed taking the events away from him."

"Well, for the record, he was a little *too* happy so I asked him his whereabouts this morning."

"You didn't!"

Morgan laughed. "I did." She placed the folder on her desk. "Okay. I'm going to go have a chat with our illustrious mayor, then head over to the competition. Feel free to go through the contents of those boxes while your searches are running and let me know if anything pops out at you." Morgan grabbed her keys and headed toward the door. "When I talked to Tess earlier about the participants, she said no one seemed all that upset about Jeff. If this is anything like the other events Bijoux has hosted recently, there are likely some rivalries worth checking out. See what you can find online."

"Will do. Where did they end up holding the carving? Since Cal was pulled as coordinator, I'm assuming it didn't stay at the Raven's Nest." JJ said.

"Actually, I heard it stayed at Cal's shop. They were going to try to move it to the community center but turns out the group setting up the haunted house had taken over the whole place."

JJ chuckled. "I wonder how that's going for him."

"He's not supposed to be involved." Morgan smiled and shook her head. "But we both know how well that works."

MORGAN WALKED to the town hall entrance, just two doors down. The police station and what everyone called 'Bijoux HQ' were housed in the same 1930s limestone and river rock structure, but a small law office had recently taken up residence in the five-hundred-square-foot space between them. She pulled the heavy brass, Art Deco styled handle and walked in. She loved the terrazzo floor with its compass pattern in the center, just one of the unique architectural features she appreciated in Bijoux. Her steps echoed throughout the two-story oak paneled main hall, with offices spanning on both sides. She headed toward the mayor's at the end on the right.

Todd the Security Guard glanced up from his crossword puzzle. "Oh, hey, Captain. How goes it?"

Morgan smiled as she walked past the desk. "It goes, Todd."

Bobby Hayes, Ed's assistant, greeted Morgan as she entered the office. "Oh, hi Captain. What can I help you with?"

"I need a moment with the mayor, please."

"Let me check his schedule. You know how busy he is with the upcoming election."

Morgan leveled her gaze at Bobby. "He'll want to make time for this chat."

Bobby shrunk a little under Morgan's stare. "I'm almost afraid to ask but did something bad happen again in our beautiful little town?"

Morgan ignored the question. "I need to talk to Ed." She looked pointedly at the appointment book on Bobby's desk. Bobby and Ed were both old school, liked to write things down rather than keep an electronic schedule.

Bobby looked from Morgan to the calendar. "I'm not seeing any openings today but let me check with him." Bobby jumped up from his desk and scurried down the hall to Ed's office. He returned just as quickly.

"Mayor Peltier will see you now."

Morgan headed down the short, carpeted corridor and entered Ed's office. Everything here said Look At Me—from the vast collection of framed photos of Ed himself with random politicians and semi-celebrities doing things around town, to the large mahogany desk in the center of the room, to the ostentatious display of trophies, various awards, and gifts from visiting dignitaries.

Ed was writing something in his calendar but pointed at one of the antique hand carved chairs opposite his desk. "Have a seat." When Morgan didn't sit, he glanced up, then leaned back in his chair. "I know that look. Nothing good ever comes of that look. We're just five days away from the election, you know."

Morgan stared down at the mayor. Maybe JJ was right. Cal would at least show some sort of empathy rather than worry about how a murder would look for his reelection campaign. Or so she hoped. "If you know the look, then you know the election is the last thing I'm thinking about." She blew out a breath. "One of the carving contestants was found dead this morning out at Gourds Galore. Just wanted to give you a heads up." Ed looked like the proverbial deer caught in the headlights. When he didn't immediately respond, Morgan added. "I'll keep you posted."

"Wait a minute." Ed stood and walked over to the large window overlooking Main Street. "I took the event away from Cal. People are going to think this is my fault now." He turned to face her, and she saw fear in his eyes.

"I don't know what to tell you. My job is keeping the town and its people safe, not tracking the polls."

"Like I said, the election is only five days away." He scratched his balding head. "I have to get reelected. I mean, what am I going to do if lose?"

"What did you do before you were mayor?"

"I've been in this office so long, it's hard to remember life before." Ed dropped into his large brown leather desk chair. "I bartended my way through law school. I suppose I could practice law again. I'll still be the judge since that's an appointment by the county chair and has nothing to do with being mayor." He glanced around his office. "But I really enjoy this job and I'm not about to lose it over another dead body. Solve the case, Captain, before the election. Please."

"I'll do everything I can, but no promises." Morgan headed out the door, then stopped and said over her shoulder, "His name was Jeff. Compassion for the dead person might help your campaign, you know. The public appreciates humanity from their politicians so you might want to think about that when you're out stumping for votes."

CHAPTER 7

MORGAN LEFT town hall and started walking the half mile or so down Main Street, toward the Raven's Nest bookstore. Lake Michigan was a couple of blocks behind her, but she could still hear the beating of the waves against the shoreline. She loved the tangy scent of the water, that hid who knew how many secrets, as it carried toward her on the wind.

The town certainly embodied the spirit of Halloween, with each shop decorated with skeletons, orange and black banners and ribbons, twinkling lights, witches, and pumpkins. She smiled. Bijoux took pride in its moniker as Most Haunted Town on Lake Michigan. This was her first Halloween since returning to her hometown and she hadn't realized how much she'd missed it. Her mom, Billie, was all about Halloween when Morgan was growing up. Even after her parents divorced, her mom would always get an early start on decorating the beach around their cottage with grinning jack-o-lanterns. She always said they scared bad luck away.

Thoughts of her mom always brought a mixed bag of emotions, sadness leading the pack. She'd been gone a few years now, but Morgan believed she'd be happy knowing her daughter was back in Bijoux. "And, somehow, I think you do know I'm here. Miss you mom," Morgan whispered to the wind.

"Hey, Morgan! You got a minute?" Wendy Peltier, Mayor Ed's fifty-ish younger sister, knitter extraordinaire, and newer town resident, was waving at Morgan from her yarn shop across the street.

Morgan shook off her reverie as she made her way over to Wendy's Whimsies. Wendy was wearing a beautiful black sparkly shawl with a bat pattern. One of her own creations, no doubt. "This is fun," Morgan said, pointing at the wrap and smiling.

"Thank you. I just finished writing up the pattern last night." Wendy beamed. "Creating something out of nothing is one of my passions. Well, besides the store, of course."

"It's gorgeous and you're obviously an artist. Is everything okay? Is there something I can help you with?"

"Actually, yes, there is one thing. We haven't had a chance to talk much since I moved here and set up shop, but in addition to fiber arts," she flipped the end of the shawl, "I also teach yoga. I've decided to do a series of special introductory classes to coincide with the Pumpkins and Poe Festival. Thought it'd be a fun way to get folks into the shop and studio." Wendy smiled and tucked a strand of silver brown hair behind an ear. "Please consider yourself invited. And anyone else you'd like to bring along."

"You know, I've had several friends try to get me to a yoga class. They all thought it would help with the stress of the job. Honestly, I don't know if it's my thing, putting my body in positions it wasn't intended to be in."

"You're not the first person to say that." Wendy laughed. "If it helps any, I'm a firm believer in listening to the body and not forcing it to do painful things, especially when we're on the mat. Tell me, what do you do to relax now?"

Morgan grinned. "Ride my motorcycle. It's the best way I know to unwind."

"I love that. But how about we find another way for you to chill? It's not like you can ride in the winter," Wendy offered. "Right? On the mat is the perfect place to let it all go."

"Okay, okay. I'll give it a shot, assuming it works with my current schedule." Morgan sighed. She was focused on the case at hand, not yoga. Or the mat. Or whatever. "When's your first class? I'll do what I can to be there."

Wendy set her mouth in a firm line. "Yoga is a commitment, Morgan. It's not something to be taken lightly." She propped her hands on her hips and looked Morgan up and down.

Morgan stared back. If there was one thing she'd learned from her dad, Able, it was to not let anyone intimidate you. She'd heard along the town grapevine that Wendy was ex-military, retired as a master sergeant, and the older woman was definitely working that side of her personality at the moment.

Then Wendy relaxed and laughed. "I'm teasing! Sort of." She smiled. "While you can join in any class, introductory ones are perfect for testing the waters for newbies like you. First one is tomorrow at five p.m. If it helps any, Cal said he'd be there."

Curious. "Cal signed up? When did you talk to him?"

"Just last night. He apparently used to do yoga on campus at U of M, said it helped keep his mind sharp, which I don't disagree with. Also, I'm helping him with his campaign." She pointed at the *Caleb Joseph for Mayor* sign in her shop window. "Can I put one of those up at the station?"

"Sorry, no. I have to stay impartial when it comes to politics. Speaking of," Morgan continued, "isn't this going to be weird with your brother running for reelection? I just saw him. He's stressed as it is. Does he know you're doing this?"

"Ed needs some weirdness in his life. Or at least a little shake up. My sis-in-law, Joan, agrees." Wendy drew her eyebrows together. "Honestly, between you and me, I think she's tired of being 'the mayor's wife.' As you know, Ed's not always the most popular person around and Joan often gets the fall-out for his actions. Which is ridiculous but guilt by association, I suppose."

"I guess I could see that," Morgan said. She imagined for a moment what it would be like to be married to someone like Ed, loud and demanding, then shivered and shook it off. *Nope.* "Hey, I need to run, but thank you for the invite. I'll plan on being here tomorrow night for class."

"Excellent. Looking forward." Wendy smiled and waved as Morgan crossed the street again and headed for the Raven's Nest.

"What have I gotten myself into?" Morgan murmured to herself. She entered the bookstore's courtyard and paused just inside the wrought iron fence, surveying the layout. The open area was set up with hay bales, scarecrows, strings of orange and white lights, and a mini pumpkin patch. Eight wooden work benches were spread out across the forty-foot by sixty-foot yard, seven of them covered with an array of tools and pumpkins. The eighth bench was vacant. No tools. No pumpkins. *Must have been assigned to Ninja Jeff.*

"Can I help you?" A young woman, late twenties with a buzzed short blonde haircut and carrying a clipboard, approached Morgan. "This event isn't open to the public yet."

Morgan extended her hand. "I'm Morgan Hart, the police captain. And you are—?"

"Ella. Ella Birch." She shook Morgan's hand. "I'm with the production group for the online show and event sponsor, *Astounding Pumpkins*."

"I didn't realize this was a televised event."

"Oh, it's not, actually. There's a group of us who help manage the event for whatever town is hosting. We also film and photograph the carvers for our website and other social media outlets. I'm in charge of establishing the set and getting the shots." Ella beamed. "And I'm proud to say we have over two million followers. It's how we were able to bring in this year's fifty-thousand-dollar prize. But I imagine that's not why you're here."

"You'd imagine correctly. Have you heard about Jeff Malone?"

"I did. Sinclaire and Jimmy informed us he was gone." She hung her head. "It's just terrible."

"Did you know him?" Morgan asked.

"Sort of. I've only been part of the show for a little over a year, but Jeff was around the carving scene much longer than that. He's one of the OGs," Ella said. "OG stands for old guy."

"Yeah, I know what it means." *How old does she think I am?* Morgan walked around the empty work bench, ran her hand around the edges and underside. *Nothing here.* She straightened. "What can you tell me about him? Any recent issues he may have been dealing with?"

"Wait. I thought he died from falling and hitting his head, but you're making it sound like he was he murdered."?

"Captain Morgan wouldn't be here if it was a simple accident," Cal said as he walked up.

Morgan turned. "You're not supposed to be out here."

Cal bristled. "I can be out here. This is my property. I'm simply not allowed to be part of the event, or any other town-wide event." He tugged at the deep green sweater he wore over dark jeans.

"No need to get your knickers in a twist."

"You did not say knickers." Cal burst out laughing.

Morgan grinned. "I've been saving that one, just for you."

Ella looked from Morgan to Cal and back to Morgan. "Did you need anything else from me, Captain? The competition starts in about an hour and we're still getting things ready."

"Just one more question for now. Have you heard any talk among the other competitors about Jeff or his death?"

"Word on the street is there was infighting going on with some of Ninja Jeff's groupies." Ella sighed. She leaned in and whispered, "I heard he was a serial dater, had his pick from his followers. He also liked to post stuff on social media about his competitors, questioning their talent. He even took jabs at their fans."

"It sounds like Jeff liked to stir things up."

"Let's back up a minute. Pumpkin carvers have *groupies*?" Cal asked. "Like *The Grateful Dead*?"

"Of course, they do. You sound surprised. The top ones, which I believe we've managed to pull together for this festival, have upwards of over a million followers online between the eight of them." She frowned. "Well, seven. We won't be able to replace Jeff this late in the game. Not that he's replaceable. Despite rumors of fighting other carver's and their fans and being generally irritating, he still seemed like one of the good guys."

Morgan wondered for a moment what one of the bad guys was like. "What time did you say you start today?"

Ella checked her phone. "4 p.m. Little over an hour."

She handed Ella one of her cards. "I'll be back but please reach out if you hear anything before then."

"Hey, Ella! Where d'you want this skeleton?" a young man called from the makeshift pumpkin patch.

"Will do. I have to go."

Morgan watched for a moment as the other woman hurried off and helped attach the prop to a tree. She turned the idea of pumpkin groupies following their favorite carvers around in her mind. *Who knew?*

"Would you like to come inside and have some coffee while you're waiting for the start? I just brewed a fresh pot," Cal offered.

"That's about the best thing I've heard so far today." Morgan followed Cal into the Raven's Nest. Walking into the bookstore always brought back memories of her childhood and the time she spent here with Cal's uncle, Baptiste St. Aubien. The gruff old man had been like a grandfather to her. He'd left Cal the shop when he passed. The bookstore was busier than usual with the festival starting tomorrow night, and Billy Livernois was behind the counter ringing up sales. Morgan dropped into one of the overstuffed chairs opposite the river rock fireplace and gratefully accepted the large mug of caffeine heaven from Cal.

"Dave's special blend from the deli, Halloween Chocolate Darkness." He sat down, then took a sip. "And it does not disappoint."

"I love that he's started roasting his own coffee." She sipped and smiled. "You're right. It's delicious." Morgan cradled the mug in her lap.

Cal rested an arm on his knee and leaned toward Morgan. "I take it we do have a murder on our hands?" he whispered.

Morgan glanced around her. The seating area was off to the side, and no one seemed to be paying any attention to them. She looked at Cal and frowned. "We do. Jeff was asphyxiated with a pumpkin."

Cal blew out a low whistle. "That's a hell of a way to go."

"My working theory is he was incapacitated by the head wounds and either someone took advantage of the situation or caused the wounds to begin with, then finished the job with a pumpkin." Morgan took another drink of coffee. "JJ and I are just getting started with the investigation, so we really don't have much now. It sounds like the victim wasn't all that nice of a guy."

"If you irritate the right person enough times, it could definitely come back to haunt you," Cal said.

CHAPTER 8

MIRANDA MELODY DANIELS, one of the goth teens who protested pretty much everything in town, burst into the Raven's Nest. "It's horrible and it's happening!"

Morgan and Cal set their cups down and rushed to her side. Morgan touched her shoulder and gave her a quick once over. She seemed physically okay but was obviously distraught. "What's happening? What's wrong, Miranda?"

"The witches! The Bijoux Witches are here and they're fighting for control!"

Morgan stepped back. "Okay, let's back up a second. What are you talking about?"

"There's no time for explanations," Miranda huffed. "They're out at Lac Voo Nature Preserve, dueling over who gets to claim the soul of our beloved lake monster, Messie."

Messie was the creature of legend who supposedly inhabited Lake Michigan, protecting good townsfolk and destroying the boats of pirates. Messie lived by a sacred code, which Morgan could definitely relate to, if Messie actually existed. "You do know there's no such things as lake monsters, right?" Morgan crossed her arms. "Or witches, for that matter. We've been through this."

"Messie would never appear for you, with your negative vibes and naysayer attitude." Miranda made a face and blew a strand of bright blue hair out of her eyes. "It's why you didn't see her when the psychics were here. She *senses* how you feel about her, and it makes her so sad." The teen sniffed and wiped at her nose with the back of her hand. "For real."

Fighting witches. Sad lake monsters. Pumpkin groupies. A dead carver. It was stacking up to be a helluva day. Whatever was going on at the preserve was likely more kids working on Halloween pranks but maybe, just maybe, it might have something to do with the murder. Stranger things were known to happen, but in the town of Bijoux, they seemed to happen on a regular occurrence. Morgan checked her smart watch. "Fine, I have a little bit of time before the contestants arrive. I'll take a ride out and see what's going on." Morgan glanced at Cal. "I assume you're coming with me?"

Cal turned to Billy who was just finishing up with a customer. "Hey, Billy, I'm going to run out for about forty-five minutes. Are you okay to watch the shop?"

Billy grinned and shot Cal a thumbs up.

Cal's eyes met Morgan's. "Wouldn't miss it."

MORGAN AND CAL took M-22 north to the Lac Voo Nature Preserve a few miles up the road. The preserve covered roughly fifteen square miles, including Lake Michigan frontage, and had been deeded to the sister towns of Bijoux and Lac Voo in 1953 by one of the wealthy wine country families. Bijoux sat on one side of the grounds and Lac Voo, on the other.

"What's the deal with the Bijoux Witch thing Miranda was talking about?" Morgan asked. "I never heard of that when I was a kid."

"It's relatively new, only goes back about ten years," Cal explained. "A local coven decided to have their Samhain celebration out there and someone came across them, assumed there were nefarious acts afoot and called your dad in, since he was police captain at the time." Cal rolled down the window and rested his elbow on the sill. "Of course, it was nothing more than some moonlight dancing around a fire, but you know how it is around here. Next thing you know, we have evil witches haunting the preserve every October."

"Nefarious acts?" Morgan laughed. "Okay, then. I'll ask dad about it later if it turns out to be anything." She turned the truck onto the gravel road leading to a parking area near the front of the preserve and parked. She stared out over the grounds for a moment. "I loved coming here when I was a kid. Now all I can think about is that the first murder in Bijoux in almost a hundred years occurred out here on my very first day on the job. And then another murder. And even more murders." She shook her head. "It's crazy."

"I know you're doing everything you can to keep bad things from happening." Cal put his hand over hers where it rested on the steering wheel. "And, if it's any consolation, none of the recent wave of murders had anything to do with the townspeople of Bijoux. They were all from out of town. The perpetrators would have likely committed the murders no matter what city or town they were in. So, there's that."

Morgan pushed down the uneasy twinge in her stomach and nodded as they exited the truck. "Yeah, there's that."

"Shall we search for some witches?" Cal asked.

"Let's head down to the shoreline. If there's anyone out here trying to conjure lake monsters, makes sense that's where they'd be."

"Good deductive reasoning," Cal said. "I like how you think like a cop."

"Because I am a cop. Or did you forget that?"

Cal held a stand of beach grass aside that was blocking the path to the beach. "I find the way you process thoughts interesting, that's all. It's been very helpful with developing my homicide detective character, Philip McDonald."

She shot him a look out of the corner of her eye. "Glad to be of service." A movement ahead caught her attention. There were three tents set up about twenty feet from the shore, on the beach just outside the vegetation line, and three people were sitting around a driftwood fire. They glanced up when Morgan and Cal entered the clearing.

"Yeah? You want something?" a mid-twenty-something woman, with bright green braids scattered in her blonde hair, asked.

"Be nice, Bridget," another woman, late twenties, regular brown hair, said. She stood. "I'm Toody Hawk. And, based on your uniform and that gun on your hip, you must be the police. Or at least, I hope that's the case."

"I'm Captain Morgan Hart. Cal here is a sidekick." Morgan smiled.

"Now wait a minute," Cal said. "JJ is the side kick. We've already determined this."

"No, you've determined that." Morgan turned back to Toody. "Are you vacationing?"

The group laughed. "No, not at all. We're working. We follow the pumpkin carvers around. It's a full-time job this time of year," Toody said.

Huh. So pumpkin groupies were an actual thing. Remembering what Ella had shared, Morgan asked, "Are you here for a specific carver, or just carvers in general?"

"Oh no, the followers all have their favorites," Bridget said. "Usually."

"Mine's Ninja Jeff. No one can wield a knife like that man." Toody heaved a deep sigh. "Or at least, he used to be. We heard on the news about his death."

The third woman snorted.

"Anything you want to add?" Morgan asked.

"Jeff wasn't a good person so I'm not sad, that's all."

"And you would be—?"

"Nancy Malone." She was a red head and little older than the other two. She glanced around the circle at the other women, who Morgan noticed were glaring at her. "All of us were married to Jeff. He was our husband."

"Wait a minute," Cal interjected. "*Our* husband? Consecutively, right?"

"Nope, not consecutively. Like I said, he wasn't a good person. We found out at a carving event last week he'd wed us all without divorcing the others. We thought we'd all meet up here and have a conversation with him." She shrugged. "Though I am—was—the first wife, so the only one who actually counts."

"We have not established that," Bridget said.

Nancy snorted. "Oh, please. I knew Jeff when he was just starting out. You two didn't show up until well after he'd made a name for himself." She pointed at herself. "I'm the original Mrs. Ninja. Y'all are just wannabes."

Bridget stood and she and Toody took a step toward Nancy. Morgan intervened. "Hold on. Everyone sit back down." She pulled a notebook from her back pocket. "Where were each of you early this morning, between six and seven a.m.?"

The trio looked at each other but none of them replied.

"Look, we can talk out here or we can all go into town and have this conversation at the police station."

Nancy opened her mouth and hesitated when Toody and Bridget shook their heads at her. "We were here," she finally said. "Hanging out, doing stuff around the fire." She shrugged. "General witchy hijinks."

"Excuse me," Morgan said, "But what exactly does that mean, *witchy hijinks*?"

"You shouldn't have said anything, Nancy." Bridget ground the words out. "It's not their business if we practice the craft."

"Considering you've all just told me you came here this weekend to confront Jeff, were married to him at the same time, and he's now dead, I'd say that makes it my business."

Bridget snorted. "You can't be seriously accusing any of us of killing him."

"I don't want to go into any details," Nancy said. "Suffice to say we were all here, on the beach, at the same time."

"Which makes you each other's alibis," Cal said. "Convenient."

"Wait," Toody said. "There was a nosy girl out here. Maybe seventeen. I noticed her blue hair. She was spying on us through the beach grass but was only there for a few minutes, so we didn't worry about it too much."

Cal looked at Morgan and they both said, "Miranda."

Morgan's phone pinged a text message from JJ. *Posts and tweets confirm no love lost between the carvers. One stands out, though. Vic the Viper. He's in town this weekend. Haven't found anything damning about Sinclaire or Jimmy but still digging.*

Vic the Viper? Ninja Jeff? What was it with the stage names? It's not like these people are pro wrestlers. She texted back, asking him to check into the wives. Morgan pocketed her phone and looked at the trio of women. "Can any of you tell me anything about Vic the Viper?"

Bridget sighed. "Only that he's dreamy."

Dreamy. Not helpful. "Anyone else?"

Toody and Nancy looked at Bridget with a disgusted glare. "You changed camps pretty damn fast," Toody observed.

"Hey, I was a Viper fan before I ever met Jeff."

"I suppose you're married to him, too," Nancy accused.

"All right," Morgan said. "On that note, we're done for the moment but please don't leave town without checking in with me."

"I'm certainly not going anywhere," Nancy said. "I'll be here for the entire weekend, in memory of *my* husband. I'll be watching and making sure the honor of his carving dynasty is upheld." She sniffed. "Then, I'll take him home one last time."

Nancy's comments stirred the wives up again and they started bickering. Morgan sighed and turned to Cal. "Let's go back to your place. I need to talk to a snake."

CHAPTER 9

"How's the campaign going?" Morgan asked Cal as she pulled out of the preserve and turned her truck back south toward Bijoux.

"Meh."

"Meh? That doesn't sound like you." Morgan shot Cal a look, then refocused on the road. "Are you okay?"

"I'm not sure it's worth the fight, that's all. It's challenging to knock out an incumbent who's been in office as long as Ed has."

"I get that, but when I think about how many people he's managed to rile up just since I've been back in Bijoux, seems you'd be a shoo-in."

"I would've thought the same." Cal rubbed his chin. "I've been talking to folks. The shopkeepers are mobilized against him because of the beautification projects he keeps trying to force on us. But everyone else seems to think he's doing an okay job, even though many think he's annoying."

Morgan glanced at Cal out of the corner of her eye. He was usually more upbeat about things. "You know, maybe just having an opponent will give him a scare. Maybe he'll settle down about some of his more authoritarian ideas." She pulled over and parked the truck in front of Hannah's Heavenly Confections.

"I suppose anything is possible. Why are you stopping here? I thought we were going back to the Raven's Nest to talk to snakes?"

"One snake, as far as I know. And we are." Morgan smiled. "But you obviously need a cupcake and possibly a latte. Come on, let's check out Hannah's daily specials."

Hannah's shop was decorated for Halloween with Edgar Allan Poe cutouts, bat shaped lights, and orange and black streamers. The autumn scents of cinnamon and clove filled the air. "It looks great in here," Morgan said. "Smells amazing, too."

"Smells are free." Hannah grinned and rested her forearms on the glass counter case. "How are you two doing? I heard there was an issue involving one of the carving participants. Is that true?"

"I heard Connie was already on the news with the information. And it is true. One of the carvers is dead. I'm assuming she added her usual embellishments to the story?"

"Of course. She suggested bad things are happening and you're not keeping us safe. Of course, I know better."

"Connie needs to go away. At least she can't blame the 'Detroit Killer' anymore." Morgan frowned. Ever since her return to Bijoux, her nemesis had insisted a killer had followed Morgan from Detroit. Connie wasn't far off the mark, considering the incident with James Wheat last month, but she'd never admit that to anyone. She shook her head, clearing her thoughts. "But yes, I'm investigating the death of one of the competitors. I had no idea making jack-o-lanterns could be so competitive."

"It's much more than that," Cal said. "These people are sculptural artists. At least, the best ones are."

"Agreed. I watch the *Astounding Pumpkins* online channel," Hannah added. "They're like us bakers. Everyone has their own technique and skill set and seem like they'll do just about anything to win, just as we found out with the cupcake baking contest."

Last month saw another event with more deaths in Bijoux and, during that investigation, Morgan was also able to put away her husband, Ian's, killer. It was heartbreaking and freeing all at the same time. Now, she was trying to figure out how to go forward with life. The community of friends she'd established offered amazing support; she just had a hard time accepting it. *Change of subject.* "How's the bakery expansion going?"

"Pretty good for the most part. Paul's been helping with the retail website design, as well as financing new equipment and upgrades. I'm going to be taking over the vacant space next door to build a separate kitchen and work area for catering and website fulfillment." Hannah blew out a breath. "It's exhausting and, honestly, I'm still a little surprised he wants to invest in me."

"And why wouldn't he? You're an amazing baker and a savvy

businessperson." Morgan smiled. "I mean it. He's lucky you agreed to work with him, not the other way around. Never forget that."

Hannah quirked a smile. "I suppose I have my moments..." The expression faded. "But I do miss JJ an awful lot."

"For what it's worth, he misses you, too. I happen to believe you'll work things out."

Cal raised an eyebrow. "You're getting quite sentimental, Captain." He turned to Hannah. "Having said that, I do believe most things happen how they're supposed to."

"Wow. So warm and fuzzy," Morgan said with an eyeroll. "So, what are you having, professor? My treat."

Cal gave her a curious look.

Morgan fought the urge to squirm under his perusal. Connie's accusations of 'will they or won't they' popped into her brain. *Dammit.* "Don't make this strange," she said a little more forcefully than she'd intended. "Just order something or I'll order for you." She glanced at Hannah, who was watching them both.

"Fine. I'll take a Maple Bacon cupcake. But only because I'm currently under duress."

Hannah laughed. "You got it, Cal." She dropped the confection into a waxed paper bag and handed it to him. "How about you, Morgan? Something extra chocolatey to make your day better?"

"I'm not sure there's enough chocolate to improve this day. Having said that, I'll take one of your Triple Chocolate Mochaccinos."

Cal gave her a raised eyebrow look.

"What?" she huffed. "It certainly can't hurt."

MORGAN POPPED the last of her cupcake into her mouth as she pulled up along the curb outside The Raven's Nest. She put the truck in park and started to exit, but Cal just sat there. She turned to him. "Now what?"

"I'm wondering how you want to handle the snake questioning, since JJ isn't here. Should I be the good cop or the bad cop?" He adjusted his black horn-rimmed glasses. "Maybe I should be the bad one this time. People already assume you're the bad one, so it would be an interesting twist."

"They do not assume that. And your question is easy to answer. You will be *no* cop."

Cal sighed. "I was really hoping to step into the shoes of Detective Philip and flex my own investigative muscles."

"Do it on your own time, not mine," Morgan said as she climbed out of the truck and slammed the door.

He walked around to where Morgan was standing. "Fine. But know that you're hindering my artistic expression."

Cal hung his head slightly and Morgan wondered if he was truly upset or feigning it. She decided to go with what she knew. "Stop playing me. I'm onto you and it's not going to work this time."

"No idea what you're talking about, Captain," he said, but Morgan noticed his eyes were sparkling and she was reminded of a tall, dark elf. Or maybe a goblin. It could go either way with this man.

The pair entered the back courtyard. The first round of competition was underway with seven benches occupied with carvers and bits and pieces of pumpkin flying everywhere. Morgan motioned to Ella.

"Did you need something?" the younger woman asked.

"I'm looking for Vic the Viper."

"He's over there, the one dressed in all black."

Morgan followed where Ella pointed. "They're all dressed in black."

"Oh, I suppose they are. He's the one with the snake tattoo wrapped around his bald head."

"Ah, I see. Thank you," Morgan said and started to walk over to Vic's station.

Ella stepped in front of her. "Where do you think you're going?"

"To question him."

"Sorry, no can do. We're filming and we're in a timed event right now, the *Jack Amok*. They have to each come up with an original jack-o-lantern design based on Poe's *The Tell Tale Heart*. You know, in keeping with the festival theme." Ella looked out over the yard. "The two lowest scores will be eliminated."

"You're not serious."

"Of course, I am. Pumpkin carving is serious business." She checked her watch. "Time's up in fifteen minutes. Can you please wait until then? Oh, and after our round of judging? We brought in the best judges for this competition." Ella motioned with her head to the table at the front where three people sat. "That's Showoff Sal, Ricky Rock n' Roll, and you know Tess Clooney."

"No interesting nicknames for Tess?"

Ella wrinkled her nose. "Of course not. She's not a carver."

It was the cupcake baking contest all over again. Morgan scowled. "Fine." She looked over at Cal, who was standing to her right, and still holding the bag with the maple bacon cupcake. "You going to eat that?"

He straightened. "Eventually. For now, it's going back inside with me. I have a box of early editions of Edgar Allan Poe books to sort. Interested in a distraction until you can talk to the snake?"

"Viper. And yes, you know Poe is one of my favorites!" She looked over at Ella and said, "I'll be back in twenty."

CHAPTER 10

MORGAN RAN a hand over the cellophane encased second edition copy of *The Murders in the Rue Morgue,* a tribute volume published several years after Poe's death. "If my dad hadn't been a cop, this story likely would have moved me in that direction."

Cal looked over her shoulder and commented, "This particular work is considered to be the first mystery novel ever written. Poe sparked an entire genre with *Murders*."

"Exactly. The whole idea of an orangutan committing those crimes is, of course, completely absurd. But it's the absurdity of the situation that attracted me."

"How so?"

"It helped me to understand that things are almost never what they seem."

"An astute observation." He took the book from her, looked it over, then handed it back with a smile. "It's yours."

"I couldn't. It's worth too much."

"To hear the wonder in your voice is priceless to me."

Their eyes met and held.

Will they, or won't they?

Morgan was the first to break away. "Thank you. I'll cherish it."

"Captain Morgan!" Billy, Cal's helper at the store, shouted. "They're fighting out in the courtyard!"

Morgan ran out, with Cal and Billy and the few folks who'd been in the bookstore close behind. Two carvers were squared off, holding large knives aimed at each other, fencing style.

"I'm the winner. You cheated," one of the men ground out the words.

The other snorted. "How do you cheat when everyone is here, watching? You're delusional, as usual."

"What's going on, guys? How about you two put those knives away," Morgan said as she cautiously approached the pair. They reluctantly obeyed, placing their knives back on their work tables, but continued to eye each other as if they'd pounce if either were provoked.

Sinclaire rushed up to Morgan, her cat carrier slung over her shoulder. "I saw everything. Gary Ghoul here was trying to sabotage Beck the Beast." A Siamese cat howl emanated from the carrier, the kind that sounds like a baby crying. Sinclaire peered into the cage. "Hebrides agrees. He does not like cheaters."

"Mind your own business," Gary ground out. "Unless you want me to come looking for that cat of yours."

Sinclaire hugged the caged Siamese to her. Tears formed in her eyes as she looked at Morgan.

"You just bought a visit to the police station, Mr. Ghoul," Morgan said. She pulled her cell out and texted JJ. *Come on over to the Raven's Nest. One to take in. So far.*

"That's ridiculous. I didn't do anything."

"You threatened another contestant with a knife. And Sinclaire's cat." Morgan motioned for him to spin so she could secure his hands.

"What about Beck? He had a knife, too."

Morgan looked over at the other man who, she noticed, was watching her movements a little too intently. The other carvers had also surrounded him in what appeared to be a show of solidarity. After she had Gary settled, she approached Beck. "Tell me what happened."

"Gary Ghoul is a sore loser," one of the carvers said.

"He's known for dulling knives when someone steps away from their station," Jimmy offered. "We all keep an eye on him when he's competing."

"Is that what happened to you?" Morgan asked Beck.

He frowned. "Not only that, but I'm also missing my *favorite* knife." He glared over at Gary. "I just know he has it somewhere."

Morgan looked the crowd over. They seemed to agree with Beck the Beast over Gary Ghoul. *I'll never get used to these names.* All, it seemed, except for Vic the Viper, who was standing just a few steps away from the other competitors, his hands clasped behind his back.

"How can I help, Cap'n?" JJ asked as he strode up. He glanced at the well weathered bench where she'd deposited Gary. "That the one I'm taking in?"

Ella stepped forward, followed closely by Tess. "You can't take him yet. We haven't had the judging."

"Please, Morgan," Tess added. "It'll only take a few minutes and, really, it's not like he's going to win. I mean, did you see that pumpkin of his?" She snorted.

"Hey," Gary said. "Everyone has an off day."

"Fine," Morgan growled. "Let's get it over with. JJ, please take him to his carving table and stay with him. When they're done, he goes to the station for a time out."

The three judges commenced visiting each carver's table and discussed their designs. Some were more obvious in their interpretation of *The Tell Tale Heart* and had carved intricate anatomical heart designs into their pumpkins. Others went for looser interpretations, like a hand reaching out through the floorboards. It was late dusk and all the pumpkins, lit from within, cast an eerie glow around the courtyard. After talking to the contestants, the judges went off to the opposite side of the yard to deliberate.

"A murder and a knife fight and I'm not the host. Imagine that," Cal said from behind Morgan.

Morgan turned to face him. The man had a smile a mile wide. "Oh please. Get over it. Nobody likes a gloater."

Cal continued to smile.

The judges returned to their seats and the carvers assembled in a straight line in front of their table. "Tonight's winner, with their reverberating heart pattern which actually dripped fake blood, is Phantom Fred."

Everyone clapped and Fred offered a bow with a flourish. "Thank you." He put a hand on his pumpkin. "I'm honored."

Tess stood. "Now for the eliminations. I don't think it'll come as a surprise to anyone that Gary Ghoul is out." She looked over at the man. "We checked Beck's knives and they were, indeed, dulled. We do not tolerate cheaters."

Gary started to protest, then must've thought better of it because he snapped his mouth shut. It probably helped that JJ was standing right next to him.

"And the other elimination tonight goes to Beck the Beast. It had nothing to do with the fight, Beck," Tess said. "Your *Tell Tale* heart was more Valentine than Halloween and the other carvers were just better today. You can both pack up your kits."

While JJ worked with Gary to get his tools loaded up before he took him back to the station, Morgan approached Vic the Viper. "Congratulations on not getting eliminated."

"It's a given. I'm the best one here."

"I'd say there are four other people still competing who would disagree." Morgan glanced around the area. "But that's not why I'm here. What can you tell me about Jeff Malone?"

Vic laughed. "Ninja Jeff? Has-been. He was on his way out."

"What makes you say that?"

"Look at the work he was doing lately. It's all over his Insta account. Just awful stuff. He was more focused on women than his craft."

Given that the man left behind three wives, Morgan wasn't surprised. But she needed to hear what Vic might know. "How so?"

"He liked his groupies. He was fond of, shall we say, the *perks* that came along with being a champion carver."

"Yeah, you were pretty vocal online about that. Posted some pretty damning statements about Jeff and your intense dislike of him."

"He was taking advantage of those women and I didn't like it." He patted his chest. "I'm a feminist."

Morgan looked him over. About six foot, two hundred fifty pounds, shaved head with all the snake tattoos anyone could ever want. He looked more like he should be on the set of *Mad Max* than carving intricate pumpkins and calling himself a feminist.

"I'm a feminist, too," Cal said as he walked up. "People don't think men can be, but it's about equality for all, not just women. So why not?"

"Do I know you?" Morgan asked, shaking her head.

Vic grinned and offered Cal a fist bump. "Look," Vic said to Morgan. "I get where you're going with this. You think maybe I killed him. I didn't."

"Where were you between six and seven this morning?"

"The old diner in town. Dick's? Dave's? Sorry, I don't exactly recall the name. But they had a pushy waiter who thought I should be watching my cholesterol intake."

Morgan sighed. That same waiter used to worry over her. "That would be Jerome. I'll check with him." Her stomach growled and she clamped a hand over it. She handed Vic her card. "If you hear, or think of, anything please let me know."

Vic saluted and headed back to his station.

Cal checked his watch. "It's seven already and I'm starving too. What would you say to a plate of fried perch?" he asked Morgan.

"I'd say that sounds perfect. But you touch my fries and I'll break your arm."

CHAPTER 11

MORGAN AND CAL entered the Perch Mouth Bar and Grille and claimed two stools at the old worn oak counter. The shot gun building had booths and tables on one side, the bar on the other, and a small dance floor in the back just outside the kitchen. Francine, 'Frankie' Whitaker, proprietor and one of Morgan's best friends since childhood, approached the pair with a grin.

"Hey, kids. Grabbing a drink or a late meal?" She eyed them. "Ah, both I see."

"You read my mind," Morgan said with a smile.

"Bartender's intuition."

"You definitely have that! I'll have the usual. Extra fries, though. It's been a day and a half."

"I heard. Connie doesn't have much information, but she's amazingly good at embellishing the little bit she does have." Frankie looked at Cal. "How about you?"

"Same as Morgan but no extra fries. Still trying to save what little willpower I have left for tomorrow night's food trucks."

Frankie laughed. "You might as well just give in, Cal. Eat everything then regret it later." She shrugged. "It's always worked for me."

"Come on in, everyone! My treat tonight!"

Morgan and Cal swiveled on their stools. Tess was ushering in the five remaining pumpkin carving contestants and the other two judges. They slid into the booth and seats at several tables near the door. Tess looked up and waved. "Captain Morgan! Cal! So good to see you."

Morgan didn't miss the prolonged eye contact and toothy smile Tess gave Cal. "What's with you and Tess?" Morgan asked.

Cal looked deep in thought. "Nothing. She just looks familiar, and I can't quite place her." He kept his gaze on Tess and she randomly offered little flirty smiles.

"Mustang City Stout and Traverse Bay Hard Cherry Cider," Frankie said as she set the beverages on the counter.

Morgan swiveled back to grab her stout, while keeping an eye on the contestants. "Unless you're looking for a date, you might want to stop staring at her."

Cal's eyes widened and he looked away. "No, not looking for that." He grinned at Morgan and waggled his eyebrows up and down. "At least, not a date with her."

"That certainly sounded like an invitation to me," Frankie said casually as she walked by to wait on another customer. "Ball seems to be in your court, girlfriend."

"Seriously?" Morgan glared at Frankie for a moment. Not that the idea of dating Cal hadn't crossed her mind now that she was feeling ready to start putting herself out there again, but her friend didn't need to egg things on. She decided to ignore it and focus on Cal. "Stop looking at me like that. You can be so clueless sometimes. It was obvious to everyone you were acting interested."

"That seems to bother you." Cal looked from Tess to Morgan. "Do you want to talk about it? You know, what Frankie said. I wouldn't be averse."

"Frankie needs to mind her own business." She looked at Cal and noted the solemn look behind the teasing. Oh lord, he was serious. "Look, right now, I need to focus on this case." *Talk of potential dating will have to happen later,* she told herself. *Maybe. If at all.*

"Of course. Rain check, then. You know I like nothing better than detective-ing." He considered that. "Is that a word?"

Morgan laughed a little. "No idea. So, Tess hasn't been in town all that long. Have you heard anything about where she's from?"

"Just that Ed hired her in based on a recommendation from the governor. She'd been doing marketing and promo work for some group out west. Nothing beyond that. Which is strange considering the grapevine of gossip that flows through Bijoux."

He wasn't wrong there. Small town life meant everyone knew everyone else's business. "You think you know her, though? Maybe you met her when you lived in Ann Arbor. Possibly a student of yours?"

"No, nothing like that," he said, then reconsidered. "At least I don't think so. I'll figure it out eventually." He tapped his forehead. "Steel trap."

"Yeah, that's not the first thing I'd think to call your brain." Morgan shoved at his arm with her elbow. "But seriously, I'm having one of my own 'déjà vu all over again' moments, wondering when one of these contestants is going to explode and introduce themselves as the main murder suspect." She sipped on the chocolate-coffee stout goodness in her glass and continued to watch.

"You are not stealthy when you observe people, you know that?" Cal said, sipping his hard cider.

"Not trying to be. But, hey, doesn't this feel like when the bakers were here? I swear sometimes I feel like I'm living in a time loop."

"The bakers *and* the psychics. Both had similar situations at this bar. But then, just about everyone ends up in the Perch Mouth at some point so it's likely more coincidence than anything. Having said that, here's to time loops." Cal lifted his glass, clinking it against Morgan's.

Frankie set their fried perch dinners with sides of fries and coleslaw in front of them.

"And to the best perch in Bijoux," Cal said, turning back to the counter. "You can keep watching them. I'm going to eat."

"Food before *detective-ing*." Morgan swiveled around. She picked up a filet, dipped it in tartar sauce, and took a bite. "Frankie," she groaned. "So good."

MORGAN HEADED DIRECTLY HOME while Cal opted to walk to his apartment above the bookstore, claiming he needed the exercise ahead of everything he planned to eat tomorrow night. She rolled the idea of home around in her brain while she drove the short distance to the beachside cottage her mom had left her when she died three years ago. Morgan had managed, in between murder cases and general police business, to get the exterior painted and was now working on finishing up the inside. She parked the truck under the breezeway attached to the side of the small house, opened the front door, and tossed her keys onto the table next to it.

"Gris, Mom is home," she called out, closing the door behind her. She was met with a judgmental howl from Griselda who sauntered to the kitchen from a back room. Morgan had adopted the large black Maine Coon after its original owner, a fortune-teller who'd been in town for the Psychic Fair a few months back, had been murdered. "I know. I'm late with the wet food. But hey, I have to eat too you know."

Gris leaped up on the edge of the counter and carefully watched Morgan fill her dish.

"Here," Morgan said, placing the bowl on the floor. "Now stop looking at me like that." Morgan was pretty sure the feline would've *harrumphed* at her if she could have.

Gris let out one last mew before diving into the evening's feast of seafood mix-up.

"On that note, I'm going to bed," Morgan said. "And don't you dare wake me in the middle of the night. This human needs a good night's sleep so I can hunt down the big bad in the morning." She scratched Gris behind the ears. "You know what that's like, don't you? I've seen you stalking bugs on the beach."

The cat, of course, continued to ignore her while she ate.

"Did you get anything out of Gary Ghoul last night? Or whatever his name really is," Morgan asked JJ as she entered the police station the next morning. She placed a box of cinnamon crullers from Dave's Deli on the counter, opened it, and took one of the pastries. "Sustenance."

JJ helped himself to a treat and sat back down. "Thanks. And no, not really. I kept him for a couple of hours, then sent him on his way." He pulled a large pocketknife out of his desk drawer. "Found this on him and kept it."

"Good idea, but he probably has ten others. Did you see all the tools those carvers use? I think they have more than Dad's hardware store." She glanced across the street and noticed a line forming outside the front door of Hal's. "Speaking of, looks like a special Halloween weekend coffee cake day. Which means Mr. Dominic will likely be on the prowl for line cutters." She grinned at the deputy. "Consider yourself warned."

JJ laughed. "Noted."

Morgan walked over to the evidence table where JJ had emptied the boxes of Jeff Malone's belongings. She scanned the display of clear plastic bags containing clothing, a wallet, cell phone. Nothing out of the ordinary. "Did you go through his phone?"

"I did. Nothing unusual, though he does have a lot of pictures of himself with different women. I mean A LOT. Most were wearing Ninja Jeff t-shirts. From what I gathered, digging into his online presence, it looks like he was working on monetizing his fame. He was selling tees, tote bags, those sorts of things. All with images of award-winning pumpkins he'd carved."

"Huh. Who knew? Anything on the wives?"

"Still running searches on them. So far, I've managed to glean they're all members of the same groupie pack. I don't get how they couldn't know they were all married to the same guy."

"Sometimes we don't want to see what's in front of us," Morgan said. "It's easier to go along than stir things up."

"I could see that," JJ said. "They call themselves the Ninja Coven. Supposedly do spells and things to make sure Jeff wins."

"That could explain their self-named 'witchy hijinks' out on the beach yesterday morning."

JJ looked confused.

"That's what they called whatever it was they were up to when Cal and I questioned them about Jeff's murder," Morgan explained.

"All right then. Only other thing I've found is they really are all currently married to him. Nancy Malone is correct, though. She was the first, followed by Toody, and then Bridget." JJ took another bite of his cruller. "Who does that? I mean, I can't even get one woman to marry me, let alone three."

"Marry?" Morgan spun around. "Did you ask Hannah to marry you?!? You're back together? When did this happen?" She tapped the counter. "Spill it."

JJ laughed a little. "Take a breath, Cap'n. I haven't asked, but I'd planned to before the breakup. Bought a ring and everything."

"Oh, JJ, I'm so sorry."

"Hey, we might get back together. It could all still happen." He sighed and Morgan didn't think he seemed all that convinced. "Anyway. Did you notice this?" He picked up a bag containing a few strands of hair. "Red hair, so obviously not Jeff's. His was blonde and much shorter."

"I assume Doc is running DNA?"

"That he is. Hopefully, we'll have the results by the end of the day. Otherwise, might not until Monday since it *is* Friday."

The station door swung open and Sinclaire, carrying her companion Hebrides, entered. "I have some information for you."

Morgan leaned on the counter and pushed the box of crullers at the other woman. "Want a sweet while you tell me what you know?"

Sinclaire peered into the box. "They look delicious, but no thanks. I have an upset stomach this morning." She hoisted the cat carrier onto the counter and the cat eyed Morgan. Morgan eyed it back. "I've heard some talk."

"About—?"

"Bobby Rumble. He's the favorite to win the fifty-thousand-dollar prize this weekend. I heard Vic the Viper and Phantom Fred discussing they'd need to take him out of the running. Given what happened to Jeff, I thought you should know." Sinclaire picked up Hebrides and slung the carrier back over her shoulder. "I need to go. We start the next round in a couple of hours, and I need to get ready, but I'll keep you posted."

"Sinclaire, don't get involved, okay?" Morgan held the other woman's gaze. "If you hear or see anything, find either me or JJ. We'll handle it."

"Please." Sinclaire laughed. "I know these guys. I'll be fine."

Morgan and JJ both stared after Sinclaire as she left. They looked at each other and said, at the same time, "She has red hair."

CHAPTER 12

"YOU SAID your background check of Sinclaire didn't show anything?" Morgan asked JJ.

"Correct. And the hairs in the evidence bag are shorter than hers, so there's that to consider."

Morgan gave him a look.

"And I'll run everything again and see if I can go a little deeper."

"Good. I'll head over to the Raven's Nest and catch the next round of the competition. Maybe I can pick up some chatter." She grabbed her bag and keys and headed for the door. "You want me to get you a piece of coffee cake?"

JJ didn't look up from his computer. "Nah, I'll get some searches running then go over myself, stretch my legs. Thanks, though."

And possibly catch a glimpse of Hannah, since the bakery was nearby, Morgan thought, but didn't say it. "Okay. I'll keep you posted. Please do the same."

Morgan left and crossed the street to Hal's Hardware, where the line had grown significantly longer. Ever since her dad, Able, and his now wife, Zoe, had taken over the store, they'd offered coffee cake at least once a month and on special occasions. She cautiously approached the door, on the lookout for Mr. Dominic, hoping to evade him. Morgan glanced around. No Mr. D. *Huh. Guess he's not here.* She excused herself past the grumbling folks at the front of the line, only to be stopped just inside the door.

"Hold it right there, missy." Mr. Dominic was holding his cane out in front of her. "Who's gonna get your vote for mayor?"

Morgan squinted at him. "That would be none of your business."

The old man squinted back. The cane wobbled in the air and so did Mr. Dominic.

"Maybe you should sit down," Morgan said, pointing to the chair behind him.

"No time for sitting. I only got time for campaigning. And stopping cutters, which you always seem to be."

Morgan huffed. "I'm here to see my dad."

He continued to squint at her. "And yet you always leave with cake."

"Morgan! Come on back!" Able yelled and waved his arm at his daughter. "It's okay, Auggie. She gets a free pass."

Morgan headed to the back, chants of cutter following her. She shrugged them off. Wasn't the first time, wouldn't be the last.

Able rounded the makeshift coffee bar, crafted out of a solid core door and sawhorses, and gave his daughter a hug. "What brings you in this morning? Not that we're not happy to see you."

"I was wondering if any of the pumpkin carvers have been in, maybe shopping for new tools. And, if so, have you heard anything?"

"Ah, looking for chatter about the victim." Able rubbed his chin and leaned gently against the coffee bar. "Yes, there have been a few in here. And they were talking some about the dead guy. I don't recall any specifics but don't remember feeling alarmed by what they were saying."

"I overheard some of the conversations. Nothing flattering. He didn't seem to be very well liked," Zoe added from where she stood on the other side of the coffee bar. She handed Beau Cornet, Morgan's former high school flame and now town butcher, a slice of pumpkin chocolate chip coffee cake.

"Your work is too dangerous, Morgan, what with all this chasing down of murderers," Beau said. "You should've married me. A butcher's wife wouldn't be out doing such things. She'd be tucked safely inside my house."

"Tucked safely inside?" Morgan stared at him. "You do realize you sound like a serial killer right now, don't you?"

"*My* wife wouldn't have to work, that's all I meant."

"It's not about have-to's, Beau. I like to work. I like this job. And why am I even having this conversation with you?"

Beau made an irritated face at her. "It's a shame you can't appreciate me, Morgan."

Morgan turned back to Zoe as Beau walked away. She blew out a breath. "Okay then. Can you recall any of the specifics you heard, Zoe?"

"Things like *dude had it coming*. Mostly about how unliked he was. One of the men had snakes tattooed on his head. He was more vocal than the other guy."

"Was that one leaner with blond hair?"

"Yes, actually, he was."

Viper Vic and Phantom Fred. "Thanks. I appreciate the info. Now could I get a couple of slices of cake to go?"

Zoe laughed. "Of course! Feeling hungry this morning?"

"One's for Cal. I'm afraid I was a little dismissive of him last night."

It was Able's turn to laugh. "That's never bothered you before. Could it be my daughter is growing a conscience?"

"Please, I've always had a conscience. It's just finely honed and selective as to who it lets in."

"And you're letting Caleb in," Zoe observed with one of her secretive smiles. She handed Morgan the two wrapped pieces of cake. "Interesting."

At some point during the investigation into her husband's death and Cal's help with catching his killer, she'd softened some toward him. He'd shown himself to be a true friend and it didn't hurt that he was easy on the eyes. *Where did that come from? Nope. Not having this conversation.* "Thanks for the treat. I'm sure it's delicious. See you both later tonight at the festivities?"

"Wouldn't miss it. Rennie and I will have a booth outside the shop here. Come on by for a reading." She winked. "And bring Cal."

It was all Morgan could do to get out of Hal's. She'd have to remember to take the back exit next time. Besides the questioning about her personal life, Mr. Dominic insisted on stopping her on the way out. He finally let her pass after a series of disapproving looks. He was *not*

getting her vote on account of being just generally irritating. Although, if that were the main criteria, *no one* would get her vote this time around.

She walked the couple of blocks down to the Raven's Nest. The sun was out again, and it cast a golden glow over Bijoux. Combine that with all the Halloween decorations and brightly colored fall leaves and the town was definitely ready for the Pumpkins and Poe Festival kick off tonight. Devil's Night. That thought gave her pause. In Detroit, this had been a night of randomly set fires, though the arsons had finally stopped a couple of years ago. She hadn't even considered anything like that happening in Bijoux. Not that there was any history of arson, but she felt she should have at least considered it might happen on Halloween. Morgan patted her belly and said to herself, "Getting soft all over. I need to remedy this."

Morgan walked past Wendy's Whimsies and waved at the other woman, which reminded her Wendy was kicking off her yoga classes tonight and she'd committed to going. *Maybe yoga will help.* She mentally shrugged. *Suppose it at least can't hurt.*

Morgan entered the courtyard behind the bookstore. The carvers were already at their benches and readying their space for the day's challenges. Except two of the five remaining competitors were missing. She walked over to Tess. "Have you seen Sinclaire and Phantom Fred this morning?" she asked.

Tess looked out over the area. "Hmmm. I believe I did." She checked her watch. "We don't start for another half hour. Maybe they're inside getting coffee." She smiled. "Cal set up a coffee and hot cider area for us. Isn't he the sweetest?" Tess paused for a moment, then added, "Are you two dating?"

What was it with everyone's questions where she and Cal were concerned? "What? No. No, we are not dating. We're just friends."

"Oh, good. I didn't want to step on your toes if he was your man."

Well, on that note. "I'm going inside now."

"Please tell Sinclaire and Fred to come on out. Otherwise, they're going to get a late penalty."

Morgan waved over her shoulder and walked into the store. The sweet cinnamon scent of cider immediately assailed her, and she made a beeline for a cup. Taking a sip, she turned and surveyed the stacks from where she stood. Her insides vibrated. *No sign of Sinclaire or Fred.*

"How do you like the cider?" Cal asked as he poured himself a cup. "Secret family recipe."

"It's good," Morgan answered vaguely. She began making her way down the main section of the store scanning each aisle, Cal following alongside her.

"And just what are we looking for?" Cal asked.

"Two carvers. They're not outside."

"I haven't seen any of them in here in for at least ten minutes. Billy, have you seen anyone recently?"

Billy shook his head and went back to pricing a new shipment of books at the counter.

"Shouldn't he be in school? Not running your cash register?"

"It's part of his internship. He works here during study hall." He leaned in and dropped his voice. "What are you thinking about the carvers?"

"Nothing yet. Just a vibe. I'm heading back out." Morgan stepped outside and approached Tess and Ella. "When's the last time anyone saw Sinclaire and Fred?"

Jimmy spoke up from his spot near the judging table. "Fred wasn't here when Sinclaire arrived, so she went to look for him. I told her to stay out of it." He shook his head. "She never listens. But she did leave Hebrides with me, so that tells me she won't be gone long. She's hardly ever without this cat. He's her emotional support."

Morgan turned to the three other competitors. "Has anyone seen Phantom Fred this morning?" She glanced back at Tess and Ella. "What's his last name, anyway?"

Ella checked her clipboard. "Johnson."

There were murmurs and shared looks between Vic the Viper and Bobby Rumble, but nothing Morgan could make out. Vic didn't even make eye contact. "Something you want to tell me, Vic?"

"Look, I don't really know anything." He lifted his hands, palms up, and shrugged, making the snake tattoos on his shoulders move in a macabre dance. "Could be the Phantom's pumpkins were missing when he got here this morning. Could be he went to that patch up the road to get some new ones."

"And I suppose you have no idea where his pumpkins went?" Cal asked from behind Morgan.

Morgan shot Cal what she hoped was a 'you're not supposed to be involved' look. Not that she ever really had much luck with such things where he was concerned. It was still worth a try.

Vic just shrugged again and went back to organizing his workspace.

"Okay, then." Morgan pulled out her phone and texted JJ. *One missing competitor. Phantom Fred Johnson. Sinclaire possibly missing. Heading to Opal's to look around. I'll let you know if I need you*. She started walking. "Let's go," she called to Cal.

He fell into step beside her. "Excuse me? Are you inviting me along?"

"I figured, why argue for once? Thought I'd save us both some time."

Cal stopped. "Are you feeling okay?"

"I'm fine. Stop reading into my actions. Now hurry up or I'm going to eat the coffee cake Zoe sent over for you on our way to Gourds Galore."

CHAPTER 13

"WHO ARE your main suspects in Ninja Jeff's murder?" Cal asked as they drove north to the pumpkin patch. He took a bite of the coffee cake. "Zoe's really out done herself this time."

Morgan rubbed an eye under her silver wire rimmed aviator sunglasses. "Yeah, it is good. Nothing conclusive as far as suspects go. There's obviously no love lost between Jeff and Vic, which puts Vic up there. But we found something in the crime scene evidence." She glanced at him. "Confidentially, okay?"

"Of course. And when I'm mayor, you won't even have to say that. It'll be assumed."

"I think you're assuming a lot thinking you'll be mayor," Morgan countered. "I heard Ed is giving away free caramel corn in front of the town hall tonight during the festival kick-off."

"I, for one, would like to hope it would take more than caramel corn to sway someone's vote."

"I wouldn't bet on that. Word is he's mixing it with salted peanuts and candy corn."

Cal slouched down in his seat. "I'm sunk."

"Probably." Morgan patted his arm. "You just need to come up with something better. Like your family's spiced cider recipe. That was pretty good. But you'd have to add something snacky with it."

"I'd rather not have to bribe my way into office. I do have my dignity."

Morgan tried to stifle a laugh, but it came out sounding more like a broken motor on a boat. "Of course, you do. If that's what you want to call it. Maybe you'll think of something during yoga tonight. I'm told it frees your mind."

He straightened back up. "You're going to yoga?"

Morgan nodded. "Wendy invited me. Liz and Frankie have both been after me to try it for relaxation. Thought it might be time, especially with another murder case on my hands." She turned the truck onto the gravel drive leading back to Gourds Galore, the rows of trees on either side creating a shaded golden tunnel overhead.

"You were going to tell me something and I don't think it was about yoga."

"Right. Doc found red hairs on Jeff's clothing. He was wearing a flannel overshirt and the hairs were between that and his tee shirt. The victim had blond hair."

"And Vic is bald."

"But one of our currently missing competitors is a red head. Sinclaire Wild."

"She's what, five foot four and a hundred twenty pounds?" Cal shook his head. "I realize we've seen some strange things, but I can't imagine she could've physically overwhelmed a man. But we do know Jeff was a player, so the hairs may not mean anything. If the DNA matches, perhaps it's nothing more than Sinclaire was having an affair with him."

"You did not just say player."

"I believe I did."

Morgan tried not to laugh as she pulled into the parking lot in front of the old farmhouse. Opal and Rennie Buffet, Zoe's older sister by a couple of years and owner of The Blue Crystal new age shop in Lac Voo, were sitting on the large wrap around porch, drinking what looked like iced tea. "Huh. I wonder what that's all about." She put the truck in park and approached the women.

A car pulled up and Zoe got out. "Hope I didn't miss anything."

"Just getting started,' Rennie said. "Morgan, it's so good to see you again. You, too, Cal. Of course, we all knew you'd be here today. Or tomorrow. Well, eventually."

Oh, good. More predictions. "It follows the logic of the case that I'd come back to Gourds Galore at some point," Morgan said.

Zoe sat on the remaining porch rocker. "Yes, it does. You're very good at what you do. But remember, it can't hurt to look beyond the realm of this world when seeking the truth."

Morgan looked from Opal to Zoe to Rennie and she realized all three were waiting for her reaction. She decided no reaction would be the best one. "You know me, I prefer to keep my feet on the ground. In this realm." She leaned against a porch post. "What are you three up to?"

"Oh, just doing some Samhain planning," Rennie replied.

"Samhain?" Morgan asked.

"What pagans and witches and similar folk call Halloween," Cal said. "It's one of the cross-quarter days on the Wheel of the Year."

Morgan shot him a side-eye look. "What in heaven's name are you talking about?"

"Not Heaven. Earth," he said.

"Cal is correct," Zoe said. "But finding out what we three crones are chatting about isn't why you're here. How can we help the both of you?"

Would she ever get used to the general spookiness of her stepmom? *Unlikely*. Morgan rolled her shoulders to release the tension she felt building. "I'm a little surprised to see you here, Zoe," Morgan said. "I mean, you had a heckuva line for coffee cake."

"Mayor Ed showed up and I left it to him and Able to hand out," she offered. "Like I said, we have Samhain plans to make. There are cauldrons to set up and herbs to gather and protection spells to whip up and—oh, never mind. You don't want to hear about all of that."

"People are going to think it's Ed's coffee cake now," Cal said, with a tinge of sadness mixed with a touch of whine. "That deliciousness piled on top of the special caramel corn he's passing out tonight and I might as well withdraw from the race now."

Morgan made a face at him. "You're a real downer today, you know that? As far as I'm concerned, that's the best reason to not vote for you."

Opal laughed and poked Cal in the arm. "Don't you worry. You got my vote. You're the cutest."

"Thanks for that, Opal," Cal said. "You give me hope."

Morgan made a face at him. "So now you want to get elected on your looks?"

"You think I have looks?"

"That's not what I said." *Time to back this truck up.* She looked at the women. "We're not here to troll for votes for Cal. I'm looking for two of the competitive carvers," Morgan said. "Have any of you seen either of them this morning? A tall, lanky guy and a shorter red-headed woman? I was told the man, at least, might be out looking for pumpkins."

"Yeah, I saw 'em," Opal said. "Can't be sure if it was humans or a human and a ghostie. You just never know, especially this time of year." She lifted her glass. "Saw that black-robed being again so could go either way."

"Or maybe just one of those humans was wearing a black robe," Zoe offered. Her eyes met Morgan's. "Unlike my sister-friend here, I prefer not to jump to conclusions about unknown phenomena."

Opal snorted and slapped her thigh. "Well, if that ain't the pot calling the kettle for dinner!"

Zoe shot Opal a look that said 'shut up' if Morgan had ever seen one. "Our dear Morgan isn't a believer. I'm trying to meet her where she is."

Rennie nodded and sipped her iced tea. "I think that's a good plan."

Opal continued to laugh but managed to point behind her, toward the back of the house. "They went that direction."

"Did they arrive together?" Cal asked.

"Nope." Opal wiped her eyes with the back of her hand, calming down. "You two crack me up," she said to Rennie and Zoe. She then nodded at the other cars in the lot. "Drove separate. The man got here about a half hour before the woman. Or ghost. I heard they can sometimes inhabit a body and drive themselves places." She looked at Rennie. "Does that timing sound right?"

Rennie nodded. "Seems so."

"All right then. I'll go look for our missing competitors." She glanced at Cal. "Are you going to join me or stay here and be 'the cutest'?"

"Wouldn't miss watching you work, Captain."

Morgan and Cal trudged through the back forty of vine covered rows of pumpkins and other gourds. She scanned the field. Unless

Fred and Sinclaire were lying down or hiding, there wasn't anyone here. That thought sent an icy dread through her and she intuitively started walking in the direction of a pile of large rocks.

"Do you see that?" she said in a low voice to Cal.

"Yes, but there's nothing unusual about a stack of stones in a field. Farmers do that when they plow." A crow flew in and landed on the rocks. "Although that certainly seems a bit ominous. Crows are known as harbingers of death."

"They're also opportunistic carrion birds. They'll eat pretty much anything."

"I'm surprised you know that."

"What? I happen to have a thing for corvids. But I was talking about the depression in the vines up ahead." As Morgan approached the stack of rocks, she noticed the pumpkin foliage wasn't growing in a natural pattern but had been pulled and moved in a similar fashion to what she had seen with Ninja Jeff. She also noted swatches of bright purple and blue denim underneath them. She gently moved a few vines out of the way with her foot. There was a pumpkin lodged over the body's head, but she had a fairly good idea who it was. She bent down and checked for a pulse. None.

She pulled out her phone and called JJ. "We have another body at Gourd's Galore. Please get over here and call Doc on the way." Morgan pocketed her phone.

Cal leaned in a little closer and the crow flew away. "Is that—?"

"Yeah, it looks like Phantom Fred." Morgan straightened and scanned the field again. "But where exactly is Sinclaire?"

Cal followed her gaze. "There. About ten yards ahead. Do you see the impression in the vines?"

"I do. Good eye," Morgan said as they gently picked their way through the rows. When they reached the area, they found a human form, cloaked in black, laying face down. Morgan squatted next to the body to check for a pulse. Sinclaire stirred and rolled onto her back.

"Wh-what happened?" Groaning, she struggled to sit up.

Morgan gave her a hand. "Don't move too much until we can get Doc McVie to take a look at you. What happened?"

"I'm not sure." Sinclaire gently touched her head. "Something.

Someone. I don't know. I didn't see them. They came up from behind and hit me."

"Why were you out here?"

"I had a bad feeling about Fred. I didn't think he should be in this field alone."

"What's with the black robe?" Cal asked.

Sinclaire looked down. "Wow. No idea. It's not mine."

Morgan tilted her head at the younger woman, considering her. Sinclaire had tried to insert herself into the investigation, showing up with 'information,' and then she was found conveniently unconscious near Phantom Fred's body. While the other woman's reaction appeared genuine, Morgan had been around long enough to know the likelihood of this being a coincidence was close to none. *She's somehow involved in this.*

CHAPTER 14

Doc McVie squatted down and inserted the probe to check the victim's body temperature. While he was waiting for the reading, he gently removed the half pumpkin that had been placed over the dead person's face.

"So, it is Phantom Fred," Morgan said.

"And he appears to be asphyxiated just like the last one found out here. Of course, I won't know for certain until I can examine the body. It looks like there's some blood on the back of his head, but I'm not seeing any rocks in the vicinity, like we had with the last one" He whistled. "I'll tell you one thing, Captain. Since you've been back in Bijoux, we've certainly had our share of, shall we say *interesting*, incidents. Death by pumpkin is just not something you see every day, let alone two days in a row. I may have to write a paper on this one."

Morgan stretched her neck. What happened to the Mayberry-esque town of her childhood? "Hopefully, we won't see something like this again. What's the time of death?"

Doc checked the thermometer, then his watch. "It's now ten a.m. putting TOD right around eight a.m."

"The carving is supposed to start at eleven, so the timing is consistent with Fred running out here to replace his pumpkins," Cal said.

"Captain? You might want to take a look at this," JJ said from where he was collecting evidence around the body. He held up a few strands of red hair.

They both turned and looked at Sinclaire where she was sitting on the tail gate of the ambulance/hearse. JJ had secured the black robe Morgan found her in and bagged it, so the young woman now had a plain gray blanket wrapped around her. Doc had checked her out when he first arrived and there was no sign of a concussion, just a slight bump and bruise. He'd quietly told Morgan, while he couldn't be positive without running some tests, the blow may not have been enough to knock her unconscious.

"I don't think it's her," Cal said from behind Morgan and JJ. They both jumped. "And that's how you do stealthy, Captain Morgan."

Morgan punched him on the upper arm, and he winced. "I'm doing that from now on every time you sneak up on me." She watched as Sinclaire slid off the tailgate and approached them.

"I just knew something bad was going to happen today. Like I mentioned earlier, I woke up with a horrible stomachache this morning." Sinclaire grimaced and rubbed her belly. "Truth be told, I still don't feel so well."

Cal tilted his head at her. "What did you eat last night?"

"Not much. I had a beer with the group at that local bar where we saw you. And some hummus and pita bread." She pulled the thin blanket a little tighter around her shoulders. "I'm a vegetarian."

"Do you think it could be food poisoning?" Cal asked Sinclaire.

"Where are you going with this?" Morgan said.

"If someone knew she was sick, possibly even creating the situation itself to disable her, Sinclaire would be easier to subdue out here in the field."

"That would assume the killer would know Sinclaire would come looking for Fred and what's the likelihood of that?" She frowned at Cal. "Look, I do not need you creating alibis for my suspects so just stop it."

"Wait. I'm a suspect? I didn't do it! I'd never hurt any living thing. I just told you I'm a vegetarian!"

Cal started to speak, but Morgan shook her head at him. For once, he refrained. "You were found out here with Phantom Fred's body," Morgan said to Sinclaire. "And you found Ninja Jeff. I have to consider all possibilities."

"In other words, don't take it personally," JJ added. "Everyone's a suspect until they're not, as Cap'n likes to say."

A tear ran down Sinclaire's cheek, followed by several more. The young woman started sobbing.

"Doc? Can you help us out?" Morgan called out. "Maybe a light sedative would help."

"No! No drugs." Sinclaire drew herself up and swiped at her tears with a corner of the blanket. "If you don't need me, I have a competition to get back to. And a cat. Is that all right? Or are you going to arrest me right this minute?"

Morgan blew out a breath. "I'm not going to arrest you 'right this minute.' But please don't go anywhere. And be available for questioning."

"The only place I'm going to is to carve a pumpkin." She stomped off, sniffing and muttering, "I wish I'd brought Hebrides with me."

"What's with her?" Maggie asked as she arrived pulling the gurney and body bag behind her.

"Dead body, stomachache, no cat," Morgan said.

"I will ask no further." Maggie glanced at JJ. "Oh. Hi, JJ. Don't forget we have that date tonight."

The deputy just stared, open-mouthed. Morgan nudged him with her elbow, and he snapped to attention. "It's not a date. It's two friends hanging out, eating food truck food. Remember?" he said.

"Oh, yeah. Sure thing," Maggie replied, smiling.

"Maggie? Over here, please," Doc called from where he stood by Phantom Fred. "Let's get him to the morgue." He turned to Morgan. "We'll get you his belongings as soon as possible."

"I'm guessing no word on the hair strand DNA test yet?" Morgan asked.

Doc shook his head. "Sorry. I requested it be expedited so hopefully by end of day today. Unless there's something else, we'll go ahead and get the body transported."

"No, that's it for now. Appreciate your help, Doc." Morgan started walking back to the parking lot. JJ and Cal fell in step beside her.

"I don't know what to tell you, buddy," Cal said quietly to JJ. "You can deny it all you want but you and Maggie? Sounds like a date."

JJ scrubbed a hand over his face. "Oh my gosh. It really does, doesn't it? What am I going to do?"

"I don't know," Morgan said. "But you need to figure it out. Especially if you have any hope of getting back with Hannah."

MORGAN LEFT the pumpkin patch with orders for JJ to continue his searches on the carvers and begin looking into Phantom Fred Johnson. Specifically, any possible connections between Jeff and Fred and anyone who might want them both dead. And the wives because, as JJ echoed to Sinclaire, everyone was a suspect until they weren't. If her homicide cases over the years had taught her anything, it was that you could have a lot of possible suspects, but you almost never knew for certain until a case was solved.

Cal checked the time. "It's eleven—they should be getting started with this round of the competition, assuming they're going ahead with things after Fred's death."

"Ninja Jeff's certainly didn't slow them down. And I think it's safe to say Sinclaire has informed everyone by now."

Morgan parked the truck along the street near the Raven's Nest. Connie was standing outside the courtyard gate, looking like she was just waiting to pounce. Morgan sighed. "Looks like Connie already knows, too. Might as well get this over with." She exited the truck and approached her nemesis. "I don't have any information for you at this time, Connie."

"Nothing new there," Connie said sarcastically. "As it is, I'm not here to talk to you. I want to talk to Cal."

Morgan paused. "Wait. What?"

"I'd like the mayoral candidate's take on things and how he might handle them differently than Ed Peltier." Connie motioned for Maria, her camerawoman. "Go ahead and start filming." She faced the camera. "I'm here at the Raven's Nest bookstore with owner and candidate for mayor, Caleb Joseph." She turned to Cal and spoke into her mike, "What do you think of this rash of murders that have descended on our idyllic beach town and, if elected, what will you do the prevent any further deaths from happening?"

Cal looked straight into the camera. "I would better utilize the volunteer officers and ramp up the patrolling of the town, including the stretch between here and Lac Voo, since the preserve seems to be a prime location for reprehensible activities."

Connie nodded. "Would you consider removing our police captain, Morgan Hart, from her post? It's obvious she can't keep us safe."

Morgan scowled at Connie, who ignored her.

"No, no, that thought hadn't even occurred to me."

"And does it occur to you now that I've asked the question?"

Cal glanced at Morgan, then looked back at the camera. "I acknowledge that terrible things have happened since Captain Hart's arrival in Bijoux—"

"You heard it here, folks. This candidate believes Captain Morgan Hart is responsible for all the mayhem that's settled upon our gentle burg."

"Now wait a minute," he huffed at Connie who slowly turned back around. "You didn't let me finish. I believe in Captain Hart's ability to do her job."

Connie faced the camera again. "And there you have it from mayoral candidate, Caleb Joseph. But I ask you, dear viewer, why the hesitation? Could Mr. Joseph be weighing the pros and cons of supporting the maverick police captain? Which way will the wind blow this All Hallows' Eve? I'll keep you posted on the scene as more information unfolds regarding the deaths of the two competitive pumpkin carvers, Ninja Jeff Malone and Phantom Fred Johnson." She made the cut sign and Maria clicked off the camera. "You might want to think about your stance, Cal. Morgan here could lose the election for you."

"Dammit, Connie," Morgan began, "you're bordering on slander—"

"Sorry, no time to talk." Connie spun on her heel and headed for the news van.

"I have a show to produce."

"Well, that was something," Cal said.

Morgan glared at him.

"What? I defended you."

"You made it easier for her to do what she always does." She shook her head. "Just when I thought—"

"Thought what?"

Morgan started walking to the courtyard and said over her shoulder, "Nothing. Absolutely nothing."

CHAPTER 15

MORGAN ENTERED the courtyard as the latest round of the competition was, indeed, underway. The competitors, working intently, were carving on much larger pumpkins this time around. She looked a little more closely as she walked. She couldn't be certain, but some seemed to be replicating the brick wall scene from *The Cask of Amontillado*. She approached Ella and the judges where they sat at a long folding table. "I imagine you all already know what's happened with Phantom Fred?"

Ella nodded. "Sinclaire told us. It's just horrible, really. We've never had anything like this in the five years of holding this event." She looked pointedly at Morgan. "At least not until we came to Bijoux."

Morgan decided to ignore the comment. "How did they all take the news? Anyone behave strangely when they heard Fred was dead?"

"Of course, they were all surprised," Tess said. "Sinclaire shared the details and that she, herself, was a now suspect. At that point, everyone seemed to forget about Fred and rallied around her."

"What do you think that's about?"

"There aren't a lot of women in this business," Showoff Sal said. "I'm guessing they're feeling protective of her. Don't take this the wrong way, but she definitely uses it to her advantage."

"How so?" Morgan asked.

"Oh, you know, asks them to carry her equipment for her, tote her pumpkins, stuff like that. I've gone up against her and, believe me, she doesn't pull any punches when it comes to being a competitor." He stared at Sinclaire for a moment. "She's tougher than she looks."

Interesting. Morgan glanced over at the benches where the carvers were working. Sinclaire was glaring at her. *Whatever*. "How about the groupies?" Morgan asked, nodding to the various sets of people seated in the parking lot on the other side of the courtyard's wrought iron fence. It was a party atmosphere with umbrellas, coolers, and even a couple of portable grills. Each group had placed a sign on the fence in front of them, naming their favorite carver.

"Oh, well, Phantom Fred's followers are absolutely devastated right along with Ninja Jeff's, as I think you'd imagine. There is a surprising aspect, though," Tess said.

"And what would that be?"

"Jeff's wives. Yeah, we all heard about them, too. No one seemed particularly surprised about it. And, for the record, they don't seem sad at all." She pointed to the three women who were sitting a short distance from what Morgan assumed were the rest of Ninja Jeff's groupies since they were wearing black balaclavas.

The wives, though, were all dressed similarly. In black robes. "Thanks for the info," Morgan said. She walked over to the three wives. "What's with the attire? Black robes aren't necessarily a standard ninja uniform."

"Shows what you know," Toody said. "They wear these when they're done competing. That's why we're wearing them."

"Jeff is done," Bridget sniffed. She peered out at the carvers. "Vic is still going strong, though," she added with a small smile.

Nancy tapped Bridget's arm with the back of her hand. "What the hell, Bridget?"

"Oh, what do you care? It's not like we're going to go off into the sunset as one big happy family." She wiped at her nose with a tissue. "At least not now that Jeff is gone."

"Yeah, being a sister-wife was never part of my plan," Toody said. "To hell with Jeff. He was a deceiver *and* he died before we could confront him. I'm on team Bobby Rumble now." And with that declaration, she picked up her lawn chair and moved it over to sit with Bobby's groupies. They fussed at her for a moment but, after she removed the robe, they seemed to welcome her to the fold. Evidently, allegiances were easily switched in the world of competitive pumpkin carving.

Morgan, shaking her head, left the other two women arguing and went back to the judging table. "What's the rest of the schedule for this event?" she asked.

"They finish up today at three. Judging will be tomorrow morning, then we'll know who's going to make it for tomorrow's final event," Ella replied. "The upcoming brief will be the biggest one yet and we'll crown the winner, and hand over the prize money, right before the parade tomorrow night."

"How come you're not deciding today's winner, well, today?" Morgan said.

"We like to create a build-up to the finals, so it adds to the tension. Although, in hindsight, we seem to have more than enough tension."

"We can't change the rules now," Tess said, and her voice carried an edge but Morgan couldn't tell if it was nervousness or anger. "Everything going forward from right now hinges on keeping our timing on track. Can't have my first festival event in Bijoux derailed, you know?" She turned to Morgan. "We decide tomorrow morning at ten the last three who'll go to the finals. Though with Gary Ghoul having been disqualified, and Ninja Jeff and Phantom Fred both dead, it won't be much of a judging."

"Yeah, normally we'd be sending three carvers home," Ella said. "Now it'll only be one. Bobby Rumble, Sinclaire Wild, Jimmy the Kid, or Vic the Viper."

"What is it with those names, anyway?" Morgan asked.

Sal puffed up and patted his chest. "We're creatives. What do you expect?"

"All right, then. I'll swing back around when this is done to talk to all of them." Morgan motioned with her hand toward the carvers. "If anything strange or dramatic or whatever happens in the meantime, please let me or JJ know as soon as possible."

She turned to leave and almost slammed straight into Mayor Ed. "What the hell?"

"What the hell, indeed, Captain Morgan." He sneered at her. "You're supposed to keep me posted on *everything*. Connie just blindsided me during an interview when she brought up the second murder."

Morgan bristled. "Finding the murderer is my priority, so the investigation will always come first. And that's what I was just doing. Investigating."

"Are you trying to keep me from getting reelected?" he shouted, flailing his arms.

"Are you trying to draw a crowd for your tantrum?" Morgan whispered harshly. Passersby were stopping and forming an audience.

"It's your boyfriend, Caleb Joseph, isn't it? You're doing this to help him win the race!"

It was Morgan's turn to shout. "Excuse me? He is not my boyfriend and I wish everyone would remember that!" She took a breath and lowered her voice. "Look, I was just coming to find you. Do you want to continue this conversation in front of all of these people, or do you want to talk in private?" She crossed her arms. "Your call. I can go either way."

Ed looked chagrined for a moment, then seemed to put his bravado back on. He wore it like a cloak. "Perch Mouth. Let's talk there." He waved at the bystanders. "Nice to see all of you. Vote for me!"

Morgan and Ed crossed the street to the bar and grille and grabbed a table at the small, outdoor patio. "Tell me everything," Ed said.

"There isn't a lot to tell right now. Doc is confirming cause of death for our second victim, but I think it's safe to say he was smothered with a pumpkin, same as the first one." She leaned forward and rested her arms on the painted blue metal table. "There are plenty of suspects, but one in particular is more interesting than the others. I'm waiting for DNA test results before I can state anything conclusive."

Ed sat back in his chair. "Okay. Okay. Call or text when you do have something. I can't be caught with my pants down again. Figuratively speaking, of course."

Morgan shot him a side eye. "Figuratively. Of course."

Ed pushed up from his seat and Morgan watched him for a moment as he ambled off, then dropped her head on her arms. She wouldn't miss his outbursts if he did lose.

"Hey. I brought you some iced tea, lightly sweetened with honey. Just how you like it. Also figured some fries couldn't hurt."

Morgan looked up and smiled gratefully at Frankie.

"I waited until he was gone. I didn't want to do anything that might make him prolong the conversation." She dropped into the chair Ed had just vacated.

Morgan took a sip. "Mmm..." Perfect. She popped a fry in her mouth. Crunchy on the outside, soft in the middle. "You're my best friend for a reason."

"That I am. So, scoop me."

Morgan paused from taking another drink and peered over the rim of her glass. "About what, exactly?"

Frankie threw her hands in the air. "For heaven's sake. Cal, of course. It sounded like he wanted to ask you out last night. Did he?"

"He only mentioned it because you suggested it." She tilted the glass and finished off the iced tea, setting the glass down with a satisfied sigh. "And it's not happening."

"Why not? It's obvious there are some sparks between the two of you."

"Well, even if there may have been, he extinguished them today during his interview with Connie." She dragged several fries through the ketchup Frankie had poured on the plate.

Frankie cringed. "Oof. I saw that. But it didn't seem like his fault. Connie was manipulating him. Besides, he's said the same thing to your face. I've heard him."

"Saying it to my face, in private or with friends, is entirely different from stating it on TV for the entire town to hear." Morgan said blowing on the ketchup-drenched fries before popping them into her mouth. "Also, you do realize that saying something *isn't horrible* isn't actually a resounding recommendation. You know that, right?"

"Oh, come on. You know he didn't mean it like that."

"Why are you defending him, Frankie? And I'm not buying that Connie tricked him. He's a grown man. A clever, educated man. Besides, he's running for mayor, he was bound to get asked questions like that. He should have been prepared." Morgan shook her head and scooped up more fries. "Can we please let it go for now?"

"Absolutely." Frankie gave Morgan a side hug.

"Thanks for the tea and snack. I need to get back to the station," Morgan said, standing. "You're annoying, but I still appreciate you."

"Ditto," Frankie said, standing. "I'll see you at yoga at five, right?"

"As long as nothing crazy happens at the next jury round for the pumpkins. Which, given the way the last two days have gone, craziness would not surprise me at all."

CHAPTER 10

"ANYTHING NEW ON THE CASE, JJ?" Morgan asked as she sat down at her desk.

"Maggie brought over Fred's belongings. Nothing that really stands out there. His phone is another thing entirely, though." JJ turned his monitor so Morgan could see the screen.

"Text messages between him and Jeff?"

JJ nodded. "Fred and Jeff did not like each other, and Jeff was tossing out threats in the days leading up to the festival. Things like, this is your last event, I'm taking you down, that sort of stuff. Of course, it could all just be posturing."

"Maybe. Those texts would be more damning if Fred had been killed first. And Jeff wasn't dead, too." Morgan leaned back in her chair and closed her eyes, playing out the crime scenes in her mind. "We're missing something." She opened her eyes. "What about the wives? They were all wearing black robes today, like the one I found Sinclaire in. Opal also mentioned that black robed figure in the patch before Jeff was found."

"You're thinking one—or more—of the wives did this?" He tapped at his computer keyboard and scanned his monitor. "I'm still running searches on their social media accounts but, for the most part, they're angrier at each other than Jeff. You know, I can almost understand their reasoning for taking Ninja Jeff out, but why Phantom Fred?"

"A distraction? I've seen it before when a murderer wanted to build doubt into a case, throw us off the trail so we go looking for something—or someone—that isn't there."

"Fred also had some text messages from a blocked number. Someone messaged repeatedly, asking to meet with him while he was here in Bijoux, but it looks like he blew them off."

Morgan sat up. "Can you find out who the blocked number belongs to?"

"Already did. Burner phone."

"Let me guess, paid for with cash, right?"

JJ nodded. "I am getting nowhere fast. But I'm still working on some angles. Maybe something will break once we have the DNA results."

The station door opened and Sinclaire entered, her cat carrier slung over her shoulder and Hebrides riding quietly inside.

"Shouldn't you be at the judging?" Morgan asked.

"They're still deliberating and told us to take a break and come back in thirty minutes." She started pacing in front of the counter.

Morgan walked over to the counter and leaned against it. "What's going on, Sinclaire?"

Sinclaire stopped and faced Morgan. "Look, I know I'm not always the nicest person, but I'm not a killer. I need you to believe me."

JJ and Morgan exchanged a look. Morgan nodded and JJ got up and went to the storage closet near the kitchen in the back. He returned carrying a small box. "Will you do a DNA test?" JJ asked.

Sinclaire made a face, like she'd just smelled something bad. "Oh, um, I'd rather not do that."

"You asked us to believe you. A DNA test might clear you of any wrongdoing."

"I've watched enough police reality shows to know those things are not one hundred percent accurate. Given the fact I touched Ninja Jeff, it can also condemn me." She screwed up her mouth. "Plus, what if you find out I'm related to some random serial killer? I don't want to know that. Nobody wants to know that."

"That's not how this works," Morgan said. "We'd just compare your DNA to some evidence found at the crime scene. We know you touched Jeff and will take that into consideration."

Sinclaire stood there, shaking her head. Hebrides meowed and patted a paw at the carrier door. "He knows I'm upset." Hebrides started purring and she took a deep breath and let it out slowly. She waited another moment then said, "Okay. I know I didn't do it so what difference does it make?"

"JJ will swab the inside of your mouth and seal and hand the kit off to Doc for processing." Morgan turned to JJ. "I'm going to head over to the competition. Have a chat with the remaining carvers, see if I can draw out some more info. Sinclaire, I'll see you back over there."

"Sounds good." JJ opened the kit and motioned for Sinclaire, who approached him slowly. "It doesn't hurt. And it only takes a heartbeat. Please sign this form giving us permission to do the testing," he said, pushing the paper and pen toward her.

Sinclaire signed the form. "I certainly hope I don't know any killers," she said, and opened her mouth for the test swab.

MORGAN LEFT the station and started walking toward the bookstore when her stomach reminded her she hadn't eaten any lunch, only a few of those fries Frankie gave her. She checked the time on her phone. Just enough to grab a quick sandwich. She headed into Dave's Deli, found her favorite table by the window, and slid into the booth. The TV caught her attention.

"And here I am with another of our mayoral candidates, Auggie Dominic." Connie held the mike in front of his face. "What's your opinion on the latest string of murders that's befallen our beautiful lakeside town?"

"I'm against them!" Mr. Dominic asserted. "The same as I'm against line cutters!" He brandished his cane in front of him. "And I'll deal with both of them with this!"

Audrey was standing behind him and shouted, "Stick it to the man!"

Mr. D looked confused for a moment. "But, if I'm elected, won't I be 'the man?'"

Connie pulled the mike back and said, "And there you have it from Mr. Dominic. He is against murderers."

"And line cutters!" he yelled from off camera right before the video cut out.

"You gotta love Mr. D," Jerome said as he approached the table. "That man just tells it like it is."

Morgan looked up at the waiter. "Which is what you used to do with me. What's up with that?"

"Ha! You noticed!"

"Of course, I noticed. You have nagged me since I moved back here over my food choices and how much you disapprove of them." She frowned at him. "What game are you playing?"

Jerome rocked back on his heels. "Well, Tom and I had a bet whether or not you'd notice if I stopped." He hollered at the cook, "Hey Tom! I won the bet!"

Morgan couldn't make out Tom's response, but she assumed it wasn't a happy one. "Always glad to help. I'll have a grilled cheese with tomato, please. And a Diet Coke."

"What, no fries?"

"Saving myself for tonight." He didn't need to know she'd already had some. "So, you can save your comments for another time."

"I'll have the same, but please add bacon to my sandwich," Cal said as he slid into the booth opposite Morgan.

"Why are you here?" Morgan asked as Jerome left to get their drinks.

"Hello to you, too. Why are you still mad at me?"

Morgan crossed her arms and sat back against the booth. "I'm not."

Cal chuckled. "Yeah, that's what your body language says. You're not mad *at all*."

She blew out a breath. She had more things to worry about than Cal making her look bad on Connie's news segment. Who even watched Connie, anyway? "Fine. Truce."

"Thank you. Now that that's settled, I have some information for you."

"What sort of information? And what—you were going to withhold it until I made up with you?"

"Is that what we just did? Made up? It certainly didn't feel like that." He raised an eyebrow. "It felt more like you acquiescing to allow me in your presence once more."

"Get over yourself," Morgan said, laughing. "What do you want to tell me?"

He stared into her eyes for a quick moment, then said, "I overheard the judges arguing about which contestant they're going to send home tomorrow."

Jerome placed their food on the table. Morgan took a bite of her sandwich and swallowed. *So good.* "That can't be surprising. There's a lot of money at stake. I imagine they want to get it right."

"True enough, but Sal and Ricky have taken sides against Tess. I heard one of them say she had no business there, judging the others, when she wasn't a carver." He leaned on the table. "She defended her qualifications and her right to be there, by invoking the governor's and mayor's names like that would give her credibility. Sal and Ricky have dug in their heels. Last I saw Tess, she was standing at the cider bar in the bookstore, fuming."

"If Sal and Ricky are that irritated, maybe they have a favorite and they're worried she won't go along. It probably wouldn't hurt to have JJ look into all three of the judges. At this point, it's still wide open."

CHAPTER 17

"I'LL BE INSIDE if you need me for anything," Cal said as he and Morgan returned to the Raven's Nest. "Miranda asked if she could help out here, too, so she's been covering for me while I grabbed some food."

"You seem to have a way with the teens," Morgan observed.

"What can I say? I taught high school for a few years before I landed at U of M. I know how to communicate with them. I'm cool that way."

"All right, if you say so." Morgan chuckled. "And on that note, I have some carvers to talk to."

Morgan entered the courtyard to find the remaining four competitors all huddled in a circle. The judges were walking around the table where today's carved pumpkins had been carefully placed. Some had lights flashing, others had bits and pieces rotating. One even appeared to be drizzling some sort of liquid. Morgan guessed it was representative of amontillado. She glanced around, noted the cameras weren't filming at the moment, and decided to talk to the judges first.

"Have you heard anything new about Jeff or Fred?"

Sal, Ricky, and Tess all looked up, startled. "No. Nothing. Everyone's been busy and focused on other things today," Ricky said. "Not that finding out who killed Jeff and Fred isn't important. But they are dead, so there's not much we can do except finish the competition and make one person happy at least."

"And we have a show to get done," Sal added.

"Oh-kay…Do you know who you're eliminating yet?" Morgan asked.

"We were just deciding," Sal said. "It hasn't been easy. These are all primo carvings."

"My favorite is Vic's," Ricky said. "He really caught Fortunato's horrific expression."

"I don't know. Jimmy's depiction of a hand holding the cask, pouring out liquid is pretty interesting," Sal said.

"Pffft. Trickery. I'll default to fine artistry over gimmicks any day."

"You're awfully quiet, Tess," Morgan said. "What do you think?"

"I'm torn between Bobby Rumble's depiction of the vengeful Montresor and Sinclaire's angle of a cat's viewpoint of the whole scene. Leaning toward vengeance, though, if I had to pick right now."

"Well, you do have to pick right now so we'll be ready to move forward in the morning," Ricky said.

Tess looked at Morgan. "We've decided not to draw this out, so we'll eliminate a contestant today so we can have the finale tomorrow.

"We don't want to add any more tension to what already is going on, given the loss of Jeff and Fred," Sal said. He turned to the other judges. "So, what say each of you?"

"Vic," Ricky replied.

"Bobby," Tess said.

Sal walked around the pumpkin table again, peering closely at each one. "Okay. I'm going with Sinclaire. That means Jimmy the Kid is out."

Ella, who'd been standing off to the side, approached. "Shall I call them over?"

The judges nodded and Morgan stepped just out of camera range.

"This has been an extremely difficult decision," Sal began. "You've all done remarkably well with a challenging theme and under terribly stressful circumstances. Well, except for one of you, but we'll get to that in a moment." He looked out over the group. "We have a three-way tie for first place between Bobby, Vic, and Sinclaire. Jimmy, I'm sorry, but that means you're out."

"Your technique was interesting, Jimmy," Ricky said, "but it didn't really capture the horror we were aiming for. A hand pouring liquid from a cask is more Hallmark than Halloween. Thank you for taking part. Please clean up your station."

Sinclaire rushed over and hugged her friend. "I'm so sorry."

"No worries. At least you're still in and I'll be here tomorrow to cheer you on."

"You're a good person," she said. Hebrides mewed. "He thinks so, too."

"You guys looked like you were planning something when I got here," Morgan said to the carvers. "The way you were circled up."

"Actually, we were," Vic said. "We're having a Viking funeral for Ninja Jeff and Phantom Fred later tonight, send them on their way. Competitive pumpkin carver style."

"Really. And how does that work, exactly?" Morgan asked.

"We're still figuring out the details. Why don't you join us and see for yourself?" Sinclaire said. "It might help your investigation, since the murderer usually shows up at such things."

"Let it go, Sinclaire," Jimmy said. "That only happens on TV."

"Actually, it has been known to happen in real life," Morgan said. "Where do you think TV writers get their ideas from? What time and where?"

"Eight p.m. down on the beach near that giant rock alcove. Do you know where it is?"

Morgan nodded. "I do. Thank you for the invite. I'll be there." Maybe the killer, or killers, *would* make an appearance, as Sinclaire suggested. Or maybe she was the killer and had accidentally dropped a clue.

MORGAN HURRIED HOME TO feed Griselda and change her clothes before the yoga class at Wendy's studio. "What exactly does one wear to yoga?" she asked Gris, who was watching her intently from the bedroom doorway. Morgan placed a couple of workout outfits on the bed and considered them. Gris jumped up on the bed and plunked herself down on a neon green tee shirt with black leggings. "Is that an endorsement or your way of saying forget this one?"

She looked at the other outfit. Black fitted tee and loose black knit pants. Understated and would still look good for walking around the festival. "Okay, I'm going to say sitting on the shirt means no. Good choice." Morgan switched her clothing, fed the cat, grabbed her water bottle, and headed back into town.

"IF YOU HAVE your own mat, please go ahead and set it up. If you need one, there are some in those baskets along the wall over there. Help yourself," Wendy instructed. The yoga space was set up at the back of the yarn shop, an area of about twenty feet by twenty feet, just outside the storage room. Wendy had installed a wood plank floor and mirrors along one wall. What Morgan guessed to be yoga equipment lined the opposite wall.

"This looks really good, Wendy," Morgan said.

Wendy beamed. "Thank you. It's been a dream of mine, combining my loves of yarn and yoga. Which I'm sure you could already guess."

"Well, I think it looks just perfect," Frankie said as she walked up behind Morgan.

Cal entered the space. "And it seems you're going to have a good turnout for your first class."

"I'm excited. Ten people signed up, which is about the maximum for this room," Wendy said. "Please go ahead and settle in and we'll get started."

Wendy began the class by having everyone sit on their mat, instructing them to close their eyes and breathe slowly. Long breaths in and long breaths out. Morgan could manage a count of five each direction, though she noticed others around her were still on the first inhale when she was exhaling for a second time. *How do they do that?* she wondered but before she had time to contemplate lung capacity, Wendy had them on their feet and starting poses. She called them *asanas*, but they were still yoga poses.

"Don't force your body. Let it go as far as it can. Maintain control, stay present, pay attention to your breath."

Who knew there was much to think about? I thought yoga was supposed to be relaxing. Here she was, trying to figure all these different poses, and still breathe slowly. Morgan did notice a side benefit, though. Paying attention to all those other things allowed a small corner of her brain to open up and process what she knew so far about the murders. She gave up trying to balance her knees on her elbows, grabbed her phone, and texted JJ. *Hey, can you please send me side by side photos of our victims? Thanks!*

"Ahem."

Morgan looked up. Wendy was standing on the floor in front of her, hands on hips, feet braced apart, and looking like a school librarian who just caught two students talking in the stacks. Morgan quickly tucked her phone away. "Sorry."

Wendy continued walking around the studio, suggesting various positions for the next thirty minutes or so. "Now, we cool down."

Morgan was pretty sure she'd moved parts of her body that had never been moved before.

"Time for *savasana,* so please lay flat on your backs, arms away from the body at a comfortable angle, legs relaxed. For those of you new to yoga, *savasana* literally translates from the Sanskrit as Corpse Pose."

"Seems fitting," Morgan mumbled, settling into the pose as instructed.

Frankie, laying down to her right, giggled.

"Dude, I'm trying to rest and meditate here," Cal whispered from her left.

"Don't call me dude," Morgan whispered back.

"How about we call all of you to relax and breathe?"

Morgan opened one eye and Wendy was squatted down between their mats. "You three could use some down time. Behavior in the outer world reflects what's going on in our inner world." She stood and brushed at her tie-dye purple pants. "You all have an awful lot of chaos on the brain. Especially you, Morgan. Keep coming to class, okay?"

Morgan nodded. She couldn't disagree with what Wendy said. Chaos seemed to be one of the controlling factors in her life. She moved back home to escape the fast pace and stress of being a homicide detective in Detroit, but since returning to Bijoux, she'd had three murder cases, six dead, and faced down her husband's killer. All in less than a year. *If this keeps up, Bijoux will be known as the Murder Capital of Lake Michigan!*

CHAPTER 18

MORGAN ROLLED up the yoga mat after wiping it off and returned it to the basket in the back of the studio, Cal and Frankie following suit. "I feel like I've earned some cheesy French fries with bacon sprinkles. Maybe a dollop of sour cream," she said.

"That doesn't sound half bad," Frankie said. "I'm in."

"Me, too, if we can grab something cold to drink to go along with them," Cal added.

Frankie winked. "I know just the spot."

The trio left the studio/yarn shop and headed over to the Perch Mouth. The kick-off night of the Pumpkins and Poe Festival saw vendors lining the sidewalks with handcrafted goods, Halloween-themed vintage items, beverages, and even a few games. The food trucks were parked in one section near the town hall, allowing festival goers to make their choices all in one spot.

"This event has gotten so much bigger since I was here last," Morgan said. The sounds of laughter, families calling out to wandering children, creepy groans and cackles from animatronics—all added to the ambiance of Halloween in Bijoux. "It has to be five times the size."

"Really? When's the last time you were here?" Cal asked.

"For Halloween, at least twenty years ago. Not since I was a kid. Frankie, remember that time, I think we were twelve, and the pumpkin king lost his head?"

"Oh my gosh. I'd forgotten about that." Frankie glanced at Cal and explained, "They used to crown a king and queen. That particular year, when they put the crown on the king, his head rolled off his shoulders. Everyone screamed!"

"It was the best!" Morgan said, laughing so hard she had to stop and catch her breath.

Cal shot them both a look. "It doesn't sound all that funny."

"He was wearing a fake head," Morgan explained.

"How does that even work?"

"Guess you had to be there," Frankie said, wiping the tears of laughter from her eyes.

They strolled under the old-fashioned black iron streetlamps lining Main Street. The lamps had been transformed for the weekend with plastic pumpkins over the Edison-style bulbs. "It really is just amazing how much the festival—and town—has grown," Morgan said.

"It really is," Cal said, smiling at Morgan.

"Morgan! Cal! Frankie!" Zoe waved them over to her booth in front of the hardware store.

"This is something," Morgan said. Zoe and her dad had draped the storefront awning with twinkling white and purple fairy lights and her stepmom was sitting at a large rectangular table filled with lit candles.

Zoe beamed. "It looks really good, doesn't it? So, who's first?"

Morgan grew wary. "First for what, exactly?"

"A reading, of course!" She laughed and pointed to the stack of tarot cards to her right. "All of you, sit right down, and we'll see what comes up."

"I'm in," Frankie said. "I haven't had a reading in months."

"Who are you?" Morgan asked, looking her friend over.

"What? I love Zoe's readings." She smiled at the older woman. "She's very accurate."

Able walked up and placed a hand on his wife's shoulder. "Hey, kids. Good to see you."

"Hey Dad, love what you've done to the place," Morgan quipped.

"Community spirit, honey," her dad said with a grin, "That's what it's all about. Besides, being out here helps me help you keep an eye on things."

Morgan smiled warily as she settled into the chair across from Zoe.

"Okay, you two, no shop talk tonight," Zoe admonished. "Morgan, give me your hand."

Morgan decided to play along. *After all, it is Halloween.* She held her hand out to Zoe, who held it in both of hers. A hush settled over the group as Zoe seemed to go into some sort of trance. "Nothing is as it seems. Money is the key. Follow it to the genesis to find the answers you seek..." Zoe's voice had deepened, to a low, raspy pitch. "Do not resist. Let it all go. Love will cross your threshold once more."

They all stared at her, open mouthed. Morgan was the first to recover. "Dad—"

Able handed Zoe a bottle of water and she downed half of it. "Well, that was interesting."

"What does that even mean?" Morgan asked.

"You know how it works, Morgan," Zoe said wiping her brow. "I just share what I'm told—and that one was definitely for you—and it's up to you to figure it out." She grinned and clapped her hands on the table. "Now, who else wants a message?"

After Cal and Frankie received their readings from beyond, they made their way to the Perch Mouth. Frankie seemed excited that she would be changing direction soon and Cal was equally intrigued about a coming success on the horizon, which they took to mean he'd win the election. Cal and Morgan grabbed a table outside the bar. Frankie went over to her pop-up kitchen to get their fries and diet Cokes.

"This should get us a started," she said, placing the tray on the table. "My plan is to hit Hannah's next. I heard she has a special cupcake she's debuting tonight."

Morgan sampled the smothered fries and groaned. "You need to put these on your permanent menu, Frankie. And I'm all in for a visit to Hannah's, but after that I'll need to head to the beach."

"I haven't heard of any events taking place tonight. There'll be fireworks over the lake tomorrow, though," Cal said. "What's going on?"

"Apparently a Viking funeral, pumpkin carver style." She shrugged and sipped her pop. "I know nothing beyond that but it's worth checking out. Also, take a look at this." She pulled her phone out of her small shoulder bag and held up the side-by-side image of the victims JJ had sent.

Cal whistled. "Is that Fred and Jeff? They could be brothers."

"It is. And exactly."

"Where are you going with this?" Frankie asked.

"The thought that they looked similar came to me during yoga. I'm not sure yet if it even means anything, but what if they are related and their death has to do with a family issue and not the competition?" Morgan popped a piece of bacon into her mouth. "I realize that's a long shot, so I still have my eye on a couple of the carvers as potential suspects. And there's that fifty-thousand-dollar prize they're all competing for."

"Zoe did say something about money being the key," Frankie said.

"You know I take all of that with a grain of salt. I'm hoping something will click for me at the funeral."

"I'll walk down to the beach with you," Cal said.

"I didn't ask you to."

"Didn't have to. I know JJ is tied up with whatever he's doing with Maggie, and I don't think you should go down there alone."

He finished his pop and just kept looking at her over the top of his glasses. Her stomach jumped and she forced herself to not break eye contact. "You do recall I'm a cop, right?"

"I do. And I also recall it's still good to have back-up." He arched a brow. "Krav Maga, remember?"

"Please take him along, Morgan," Frankie said. "If for no reason than to get him to stop bragging about Krav Maga."

They all ate in silence for a moment until Morgan gave in. "Fine. Fine. Just stay out of the way."

"Wendy is right. Both of your minds are so knotted up, "Frankie said. "How about we talk about other things tonight?"

"Like what?" Morgan asked as she shoved a few more fries into her mouth.

Frankie shrugged. "How about The Life of Morgan? You're ready to move on now, right, since Ian's case is solved, and it's been a few months?"

"Yeah. I mean, I think so, anyway." She squinted at her friend. "Where are going with this?"

"Are you on any dating apps?"

Morgan almost spit her drink. "Excuse me?" She dabbed at her shirt with a napkin, glanced at Cal who was watching her closely. *Dammit*. "No. Just no. Holy crap I do not want to talk about dating apps." She looked at Cal again. "Unless we discuss the professor's use of such things." Now, it was her turn to raise an eyebrow.

Both women stared across the table at Cal.

He held a hand up. "Whoa. What makes you think *I* want to talk about dating and apps any more than you, Morgan?"

"Nothing. It just seemed like too good of an opportunity to pass up."

"And deflect from your own situation."

"Well, yeah." She leaned her shoulder into Frankie and they both laughed. "What's your point?"

Cal, grinning, shook his head. "My point is, no comment. Besides, I think it's time we headed over to Hannah's to see what deliciousness she's baked."

Morgan finished off the last of her fries and pushed up from the table. "Let's do it." She checked her watch. "I have about thirty minutes before I need to hit the beach."

The trio walked a couple of buildings down, greeting friends along the way, and stopped at Hannah's Heavenly Confections. Hannah had set up a makeshift counter under a small canopy and was serving up cupcakes. "Hey Hannah," Morgan said, approaching the counter. "We heard you had something new tonight."

"I do!" Hannah quickly dropped three cupcakes into separate bags and handed them to Morgan. "Pumpkin Chai Spice with a kick of cayenne. I'm almost sold out, but I figured you'd all be by, so I saved some for you."

"I'll take one of those, too," Maggie said from behind Morgan.

Everyone turned and looked at the other woman, who was standing close enough to JJ that their arms were touching. *Much closer than regular friends*. Morgan glanced at Hannah, who looked like she'd just eaten a lemon.

"Sure." She placed one in a bag and handed it across the counter. "Here you go. That'll be five dollars."

"I got it," JJ said. As he handed the money to Hannah, he whispered, "I promise we're just friends getting food. And I miss you. Can we talk?"

Morgan exchanged a glance with Frankie, as they both heard what JJ had said to Hannah.

Hannah's face turned red, and she took a breath. "It looks like more than *just friends*."

Paul, Hannah's investor, came out of the bakery carrying a tray of fresh vanilla cupcakes. "Where should I put these?"

"Yeah, it does," JJ said, eyeing the other man. "Come on, Maggie. I'm ready for a gyro."

Morgan watched them walk away. "Nothing awkward about any of that." She handed Hannah money for the cupcakes. "My treat. And, for what it's worth, I still believe in you two."

Mayor Ed approached, holding out two bags of what Morgan guessed to be his now infamous campaign game changer. "Can I interest either of you in some popcorn mix? It's Joan's special recipe."

"There are three of us here," Morgan said. "Or are you ignoring Cal since he's running against you?"

"I'm not the least worried about my opponent," he said loud enough for everyone nearby to hear, then leaned in and whispered, "It's you I'm not happy with, Frankie. You still haven't made the improvements to your property as we discussed."

"I don't recall having a discussion. I do recall you ordering me." Frankie was what some people called a Hold-out: a business owner on Main Street who refused to comply with Mayor Ed's beautification orders.

"You still can't ask nicely, can you?" Morgan said to the mayor, shaking her head. She snatched the treats from his hand. The bags were printed with 'Elect Mayor Ed' on one side and 'Keep Bijoux Beautiful' on the other. Her watch alarm pinged. "Sorry, Frankie, gotta go."

Morgan and Cal left Frankie arguing with Ed. She handed Cal his treat bag, and they munched silently as they reached the end of Main Street where the beach began. Strolling along the shoreline, Morgan couldn't help but think how beautiful this little part of the world was. People were scattered about, sitting on blankets, sipping beverages, and watching the freighters out on the horizon. It was still just light enough to distinguish the ship's outlines against the night sky.

"How can you stuff all this flavor into such a small snack?" Cal said, holding up a kernel of popcorn. "If I don't come up with a good idea, he's going to win on this alone."

"I wouldn't worry about it. He's probably going to win anyway," Morgan said

"Thanks for that vote of confidence."

She grinned. "Anytime."

CHAPTER 19

ALL THE CARVERS from the competition were in attendance. Even Gary Ghoul, Beck the Beast, and Jimmy the Kid were there, though they'd been previously eliminated. Vic and Bobby were lighting a large pile of driftwood surrounded by stones and the others were building small wooden rafts.

Morgan noticed some of the groupies had gathered and were watching from about ten feet away, likely Ninja Jeff's and Phantom Fred's factions. Jeff's three wives sat off to the side of the groupies and were spaced several feet apart, no doubt still fighting amongst themselves. Even the judges were there.

Sinclaire, who'd been arranging small pumpkins in a ring around the glowing bonfire, finished and walked up to Morgan and Cal. "Glad you could make it. As you can see, we're finalizing preparations." She leaned in and whispered, "I made sure the disqualified carvers were here so you could keep an eye on them, too."

"The captain said you're doing a Viking funeral. How exactly does that work in pumpkin world?" Cal asked.

Before Sinclaire could reply, Vic the Viper blew into a ram's horn, sounding a loud, raucous call to attention. "You'll see," she said and hurried back over to the group.

The carvers circled around the fire and Bobby Rumble picked up a bowl of pumpkin seeds. He took a handful, tossed it into the flames, saying, "This I do in memory of our fallen brothers." He passed the bowl and each of the competitors followed suit.

"And now, we send Ninja Jeff and Phantom Fred on their way," Vic said. He walked over to the large alcove of rocks and returned with two jack-o-lanterns. One was carved to resemble Jeff and the other looked like Fred.

The three wives stepped forward, Nancy in the lead, but before she could say anything, Toody shoved ahead of her. "I loved Jeff with all my heart. And I know who murdered him." She glanced around the fire, then locked eyes with Vic. "Him! Vic the Viper! He did it."

Bridget laughed. "Oh, please, you don't know anything."

"I didn't kill the ninja," Vic said. He squinted at Toody. "Maybe it was just his time to go."

Nancy elbowed both of them out of the way. "This is not appropriate," she whispered harshly. "Ceremony now. Fighting later, for goddess's sake."

"Fine," Toody ground out.

She took a breath and continued, though Bridget and Toody were both frowning at her. "Tonight, we send our husband, Jeff Malone, into the afterlife, with protection and his favorite knife." Nancy opened the top of Jeff's jack-o-lantern and slipped the knife inside, setting it down beside the lit candle. She then replaced the top and each woman sprinkled salt on the pumpkin.

The wives returned to their seats, shoving at each other as they walked through the sand.

"That is not going to end well," Cal whispered to Morgan. "I assume you're already looking into Vic?"

"No kidding. And yes, Vic is on the list."

Vic placed each pumpkin on its own raft, in the shallow water. Both rafts had been layered with beach grass and Sinclaire came forward and lit the tinder. Once it was blazing, Vic slid each effigy out onto the surface of Lake Michigan. The carvers gathered at the edge and watched the pumpkins float away, the flames burning brightly in the night sky. Someone started playing Amazing Grace through their phone and the groupies started sobbing.

"Okay, then. That was something," Morgan whispered to Cal. She scanned the competitors faces. Most showed some sort of sadness over the ritual, except maybe for Jimmy. He just seemed bored and was checking his phone. She looked out over the small crowd. The judges caught her eye. Not one of them seemed moved by the funeral. *But should they be?*

"That it was. And an interesting idea I might be able to use for a future Detective Philip book."

"When do you even have time to write, between the bookstore and following me around?"

Cal patted his chest proudly. "I am what's known as a prolific pantser."

"Panther?" Morgan snorted. "You are so not a panther. A large house cat, maybe, but definitely not a panther."

"*Pant-ser*. It means I write by the seat of my pants, not a lot of planning ahead. It makes for interesting storytelling. I'm never sure what direction my characters will take."

Morgan considered him. "That does not match up with your persnickety personality."

Cal grinned. "Nice alliteration. And I can't explain the dichotomy. It is what it is." He gestured toward the gathering. "Now, how about this lot? Several of them don't seem to look appropriately moved by this ceremony or sad at the loss of their fellow artists."

"Jimmy would be one but, from what I've heard, he hasn't been carving very long. So maybe he just didn't know them well enough." She perched on a large rock and nodded at the audience. "I don't get a vibe from any of the groupies. I was thinking maybe the wives killed Jeff, but why kill Fred? Unless it was to throw me off track."

"The prize money is considerable. If Jeff had won, it could have been a good payout for them. Though why kill off a potential cash cow? My bet is still on one of the carvers," Cal said. "I did a little research of my own. Ninja Jeff and Phantom Fred were both favored to win."

Morgan opened her mouth to reply just as Sinclaire strolled up.

"How goes the people watching?" Sinclaire asked snuggling Hebrides in her arms. "Is being here helping you zero in on who the killer might be?"

Cal reached over and ruffled the cat's ears. Hebrides swatted at his hand.

Morgan angled her head at the other woman, considering her. *Maybe.* "Tell me, Sinclaire. You like mysteries. Who do you think killed Jeff and Fred?"

She observed Sinclaire closely as the other woman looked at each of the carvers seated around the fire. Vic was passing out beers and Sal had left his perch with the judges and was cooking hot dogs over the flames.

"It could be any of them, really. They're all highly competitive. Except for Jimmy. They call him The Kid because he's so nice to everyone."

"Have you known Jimmy long?"

"A couple of years. We actually dated for part of that time." She looked down at her cat. "He and Hebrides didn't really get along. Plus, you know, all that pressure from competing against each other, so we broke up."

Morgan's phone pinged. "Excuse me for a moment." She stepped away and checked the email from JJ. *Letting you know Doc just emailed. Cause of death for Fred was asphyxiation by pumpkin, but he also had head wounds consistent with being hit with a heavy stick or bat. Found a note stuffed in his pocket, with the word Nevermore also scribbled on it. Also got the DNA results for the victims and the red hair. I forwarded them to you. Still waiting for Sinclaire's DNA. No matches in the database so far, but I only did a cursory search on my phone. Let me know if you want to meet at the station in the morning. I'm gonna go grab some ghost shaped funnel cakes.*

Definitely. Let's meet at nine. She pocketed her phone and looked out over the water. The pumpkins were burning brightly on their makeshift driftwood rafts, casting an eerie glow on the rippling surface of the lake.

"Well, I'm going to head back to the group," Sinclaire said.

"Thanks for all your help," Morgan said.

Sinclaire nodded and turned to walk back to the bonfire, she passed Cal who was carrying two beers. He'd gone over to chat with the carvers while Morgan was talking to Sinclaire. Cal popped the tops and handed one to Morgan.

"Thanks, but I'm still on duty."

"It's after nine on a Saturday night. I'd say it's safe to have a beer." He lifted his can in salute to the full moon where it was hugging the dark horizon. "Enjoy the moment, Morgan. Have some fun. Stop resisting," he said, echoing Zoe's earlier prediction.

Morgan gave him an exasperated look. "I'm not resisting. But it's been a long day and I do need to get going. I'll see you tomorrow."

"I can walk you home."

"No need, I'm a cop remember?"

"How could I ever forget?"

MORGAN STOOD at the water's edge and gazed up at her bright cottage, where it sat about sixty feet from the shore. Her mom, Billie, had done a great job of landscaping with beach grasses and native trees and flowers. So much so, you had to look hard to even see the structure behind the vegetation. Morgan loved the privacy it afforded her while still being close to the lake.

Just beyond the house and plantings was a circle of stones and a bonfire pit, surrounded by trees and brush which had grown up during the years when Billie was sick, and they couldn't get out as much. Morgan appreciated the intimate feel the brush created. She entered the copse and sat down on one of the stones, still warm from the day's sun. Remembering the yoga class, Morgan began taking slow, deep breaths.

What am I going to do? I have a bunch of suspects, but nothing that sticks out. And the carvers leave day after tomorrow.

Her phone pinged and she checked the message. It was from Liz Shore, her former partner in Detroit homicide and one of her best friends, next to Frankie. *Wheat's jury selection is coming up in the next couple of weeks, then the trial will begin. I'm sure you'll hear from the DA but wanted to give you a heads up.*

Morgan watched the waves ebb for a moment then replied, *I'll see you then.*

CHAPTER 20

MORGAN FOUND JJ the next morning in the small kitchenette at the back of the police station. The space still looked exactly as it had when her dad was Captain. Aged maple cabinets with a faded orange laminate top lined the wall, a well-worn gray laminate table was set in the middle of the room with four diner style chrome chairs with black vinyl seats and backs. The checkerboard vinyl floor completed the old-school look. She really needed to find the funds to remodel the entire space at some point. But, for now, it was functional.

She set a to-go cup of black coffee from Dave's Deli in front of the deputy. He was staring intently at his laptop and didn't acknowledge her or the hot beverage.

"That must be some cartoon you're reading," she said. "Did *Scooby Doo* unmask the villain yet?"

He looked up, blinked, and gave her a loopy grin. "Oh, sorry." He picked up the cup and took a sip. "Thanks for grabbing this. I'm pretty sure I have a sugar hangover from last night."

Morgan laughed and pulled up a chair. "I can imagine. Which means you probably don't want one of these." She dangled a bag of donuts before setting it on the table. "Tell me, how was the date?"

JJ groaned. "It wasn't a date. And I don't want to talk about it. I mean, did you see Hannah's face when she saw Maggie standing next to me? It was the exact same face she made when she lost her dog, Gumbo, our senior year in high school. A cross between heartbreak and being so darn angry she wanted to beat something."

"I thought you didn't want to talk about it. And yes, I did. You have some major repair work to do if you really want to get back together."

"I know, but so does she. Paul was prancing around with trays of cupcakes like he owned the place. And her." JJ frowned and sipped his coffee.

"Jealousy isn't going to get you anywhere. Trust me on that one." She reached across the table and patted his arm. "Ignore Paul and focus on what you want your life to look like and go from there. Now, what do you have for me?"

"As much as I hate to admit it, you're right about staying focused. Okay, here's what I have so far." JJ turned his laptop around so Morgan could see the screen. "Since I didn't find anything in our usual police databases, I decided to drop the DNA results for both Jeff and Fred into a public database."

"The one people use for genealogy and finding potential relatives?"

JJ nodded. "Exactly."

Morgan rested her elbows on the table and sipped her coffee. "Did you find a link between the two victims? From the looks of them, they could be brothers or, at the very least, cousins."

"Nope, nothing there. I asked Doc to take a look at the results and he confirms they're not related. Looking alike seems to just be an actual coincidence. What's a little strange, though, is I didn't find any matches at all for Jeff on here."

"What does that mean? No matches." She pulled a cinnamon sugar cake donut out of the bag and took a bite.

"Basically, none of his relatives have ever been in trouble with the law or made their DNA public. To participate in these open databases, you have to upload your results from one of those testing resources, like *Find My Ancestors*." JJ scrolled down on the page he'd been reading. "But I did discover an interesting connection for Fred. He matches up with a Geraldine Walker from Au Sable."

"Walker? Like the car family?" Most Michiganders were familiar with the Walker family, who'd made their fortune in the automobile industry in the early part of the twentieth century. The patriarch, David Walker, pioneered what became known as the "muscle car." His oldest son, David Jr., was a WWII hero who died during the war. When David passed away, he left a booming business to his remaining son, Arthur. He also donated a large expanse of land along the Au Sable River to the state for conservation.

"One and the same. Geraldine's father, Arthur, continued to expand the business after he inherited it. He was grooming his son, Arthur Jr., to take the reins when Jr. died. It seemed fate was destined to repeat itself. Arthur Sr.'s remaining child was a daughter, Geraldine, and she passed away in 2019, from cancer. She was sixty-two. Arthur Walker Sr. outlived both his kids. He's still alive—ninety-one years old."

Morgan shook her head. "Sad story. Money can buy you a lot in life, but it can't buy you immortality."

"Unless Sir Richard Branson is working on something we don't know about." JJ chuckled.

"Nice one."

"Really?"

"No." Morgan finished her donut and washed it down with sips of coffee "Okay, do you think there's a connection with our murders?"

"I'm not sure yet. Fred, our second murder victim, is a very close familial match to Geraldine. And the right age to have possibly been her son."

"And you're thinking what, exactly? Fred is some long-lost love child?"

"Maybe. From what I could find in the records, Geraldine only had a daughter. Then again, rich people have the power and the means to hide plenty of skeletons." JJ popped the lid off the to-go cup and drank the rest of his coffee. "I have no idea how it could tie into Fred's death, or if it even does. I was hoping we could brainstorm some ideas."

"Okay. It's a wealthy family with long roots in this state. And, as you say, they're certain to have plenty of skeletons in their closets so an illegitimate child wouldn't be unheard of." Morgan considered that angle for a moment. "But how does that translate to both Fred *and* Jeff's deaths? You found no DNA links with Jeff." She stood and started pacing. "I still think it has something to do with the prize money. Money is one of the biggest motives for murder."

"And Zoe did predict money was the key," JJ added.

"How did you know that? Oh, wait, small town." She chuckled. "So, how about the judges? Turned up anything there we can use?"

"Sal and Ricky do a lot of antagonizing of each other, as well as other random carvers, on their social media. But nothing that stands out as 'hey, I kill people.'"

Morgan laughed. "If only it were that easy. How about Ella or Tess?"

"Ella is all over the place online: Insta, Snap, Twitter, you name it, she has a profile and plenty of pics to go along with it, including images of all the pumpkin carving activities she's worked on. Tess on the other hand, has a very professional online profile, including one of those portfolio webpages that lists her CV, which is considerable in event planning." He leaned back in his chair and cupped his hands behind his head. "Her social media is all professional too. Nothing much there other than inspirational posts, quotes, pics about leadership, and business jargon. A few funny cat pics though. But nothing personal."

"Well, that's not necessarily suspicious. A lot of business types keep a professional public profile because, if they don't, it can hurt their careers. We've certainly seen numerous scandals on that front. Think of all the public figures who have fallen from grace because of a photo or a quote that got them into hot water?"

"Yeah, that's true," JJ said. His stomach emanated a loud growl.

"Your stomach sounds like Griselda when she wants attention." Morgan chuckled. "Are you sure you don't want a donut?" She shook the bag. "Or are you now following in Cal's footsteps and trying to save yourself for the festival?"

"Did I hear my name?" Cal strolled in with a bag in his hand. "Thought I'd bring you some nourishment since I knew you'd be working this lovely Saturday Halloween morning."

How the hell does he do that? Just show up out of nowhere. And how does he manage to always look so darn good, even early in the morning? Morgan stopped herself from going down that road. She had a case to solve, and she couldn't complicate it with thoughts about Cal. *And what about after this case is resolved? There is always going to be another case. Are you going to give up on living because of your job?* Morgan ignored her inner voice. It was sounding a little too much like Zoe's message from beyond. "I just had a donut, but I could always eat something else."

Morgan grabbed the bag and peered inside. "Egg and cheese croissants. A savory choice? You usually bring sweets."

"I figured we could all use a break from sugar and try something reasonably healthy for a change. At least until the festivities tonight."

She handed a sandwich to JJ and unwrapped hers. "Speak for yourself. But thanks."

"Unlike the captain, I am eternally grateful for the non-sugared breakfast today." JJ toasted Cal with the croissant and took a bite.

"Where are we on the investigation?" Cal asked. "Anything interesting turn up after the funeral last night?"

Okay, just ignore the 'we.' "JJ found a DNA connection between Phantom Fred and the Walker family."

Cal slid a chair out and sat down. "The automotive Walker family?"

JJ nodded. "The same."

Cal looked thoughtful.

"I can see the wheels turning in that creative mind of yours. What are you thinking?" Morgan asked.

"Besides random newspaper articles, the last thing I read about them was earlier this year: Arthur Walker Sr.'s autobiography, *The Things We Made*. He lamented at the end about the lack of heirs to leave his fortune to. His only son, Arthur Jr., died at the age of 29, childless, in a small plane accident. When Geraldine was 22, she married some member of European royalty. They had one daughter but divorced after five years of marriage. Papa Arthur leaned hard on the patriarchal side of things and worried over not having a male family member to maintain their legacy."

"Lifestyles of the rich and famous," Morgan said. "Any details on Geraldine's daughter?"

"According to the autobiography, her name is Esther Ann Walker. Geraldine opted to give her the famous family last name rather than her husband's last name, Toussaint. By all accounts, Geraldine's husband was a philanderer. He died about ten years ago. Fell off a yacht during a New Year's Eve party off the coast of Monaco," Cal added.

"While this would all make for a great TV mini-series circa 1987, we need to take a deeper dive," Morgan said. "JJ, you see what you can find out about Geraldine and her daughter. And, who knows, maybe an out-of-wedlock pregnancy as well?"

"Will do Cap'n." JJ nodded.

"Good." Morgan checked the time. Ten a.m. The last round of the pumpkin carving competition would be starting soon, so she had a little time before heading over there for round five hundred and seventy of questioning. At least, it felt like that many rounds, particularly with hitting dead ends everywhere. "I need to go meet with Zoe to get my costume for tonight's parade. You guys have yours figured out?"

"Of course," Cal said. "I will, once again, be going as Edgar Allan Poe."

"You should find someone less creepy, buddy. Especially if you want to ever get another date," JJ said as he continued to scan his computer screen.

Cal looked indignant. "Says the man who doesn't begin to understand the definition of what constitutes an actual date. And, I'll have you know, Poe has legions of female admirers."

"Okay. We don't need to hear about your Poe-fueled conquests," Morgan said with a laugh. She looked over at JJ. "Let me know if you find something."

"I'm going to assume you mean besides a creepy ex-U of M professor." He eyed Cal and winked. "And will do."

MORGAN STOPPED off at Zoe and Able's house, the same house Morgan had grown up in before her parents split. It was always a little bittersweet coming here. Not that she didn't love her stepmom, it just brought back so many early memories from when her mom was alive and they were all together, one family.

"Come on in. I have some hot tea waiting for you in the kitchen," Zoe said. "And I took the liberty of pulling a few costumes out of my stash for you to look through."

Zoe used to run a costume shop with her sister, Rennie, over in Lac Voo. When Zoe made the move to Bijoux, they decided to drop that portion and focus on new age and holistic things. She couldn't bear to part with the twenty or so outfits, so she brought the inventory with her.

As she sifted through Zoe's costumes hanging on the rack, Morgan's mind wandered back to the previous time she'd dug into Zoe's vault of costumes. She'd needed something to wear for the romance writers' conference a while back while she was working a double murder investigation. Her very first day on the job, she was called out to the Lac Voo Nature Preserve, where body number one had been discovered. The first murder in Bijoux in almost a hundred years sparked panic in the town and made Morgan's investigation a tough one.

Two grand divas of the genre ended up murdered at that conference, causing a ripple of fear among the attendees and the townspeople alike. Morgan, JJ, and Cal had attended the final soiree to prevent the murderer from striking again, she and JJ in costumes provided by Zoe. What they didn't know at the time was that Cal had been the killer's third target. Before Cal launched his detective series, he wrote dark gothic romance under the pseudonym Josie Steele and was a bestseller to boot. Luckily, Morgan figured it out in time, and stopped the killer from shooting Cal on the beach.

But she couldn't help but notice, since then, the town had begun to take it all in stride, as though they were getting used to the fact Bijoux was no longer the idyllic haven it once was. That did not sit well with Morgan. It was her job to keep everyone safe and, while she didn't want the townspeople to live in constant fear, she also didn't want them to be complacent either.

Morgan came across a deep gray silk dress and paused to admire it. She held it up in front of her. "This is stunning."

"It's an actual antique, from the late 1800s, time-wise it's perfect for our Pumpkins and Poe theme." Zoe ran a hand over the fabric. "It would look lovely on you."

Morgan unbuttoned the back of the dress, pulled off her black t-shirt and jeans, and slipped the garment over her head. She smoothed the skirt as Zoe fastened the back. She turned from side to side to check it out in the full-length mirror Zoe had positioned in the room. "I don't know. What if I have to chase someone down? This skirt would get in the way."

Zoe laughed. "Just like your father, always thinking about the job."

"That I am." Morgan grinned. "Did they make ladies' dresses with pants back then?"

"Of course not, but that doesn't mean we can't take some poetic license." She rifled through the pile of clothing and pulled out a pair of black velvet cigarette pants and matching cutaway robe with a scattering of red roses printed on the dark background. "What do you think of this? Not period to our event, but still vintage. 1950s."

Morgan stepped out of the dress and pulled the pants on. She slid on the robe and buttoned the front, which fell straight across her waist in the front and to her ankles in the back. "I'm pretty sure I saw Mary Tyler Moore wearing something like this on *The Dick Van Dyke Show*." She did a spin and the robe lifted behind her. "I love it. I have the perfect boots to pair with it, too. Ones I can run in, if need be, of course." Morgan hugged her stepmom. "Thank you so much, Zoe. You're the best."

"Hey, you look great!" Able said as he walked in the front door. He folded Morgan into one of his bear hugs.

"You're just in time to join us for some tea." Zoe smiled. "C'mon, let's go sit at the kitchen table. You look like you could use a short break, Morgan."

No argument there. Morgan quickly changed out of the costume and joined them in the kitchen. The large window at the back of the house had a beautiful view of the lake. When Morgan was growing up, she would always do her homework in the kitchen so she could gaze out at the big water. For some reason, the view always helped her focus when she was stuck on a math problem or gave her inspiration when she was writing an essay.

She sat in the same spot she did all those years ago and, for a few moments, looked out the same window, taking in the easy movement of the waves chasing the gulls as they looked for bits of food. "Dad, how did you know you were ready to move on?"

Able and Zoe shared a glance. "Morgan, I'll go get your costume packed up while you two talk," Zoe said and got up and left the room.

Able reached for Morgan's hand and squeezed it. "You know I loved your mom. So much. It almost broke me when we divorced and, again, when she died. I grieved all the lost moments because that's what happens when we lose someone." He reached for his tea and cradled the cup. "Then I realized I had to move on, live life. I'd been in a holding pattern for so long."

"But you *were* finally able to, with Zoe. I always said I would be able to move on after Ian's killer was caught. But now it's over…I don't know how to let go." She sipped her tea, closing her eyes and savoring the soothing taste of ginger.

"Honey, the truth of it is, you'll always love Ian. And that's natural. Moving on doesn't mean you have to forget him or let go of your love —it just means opening your heart to let a new love in." He smiled at her. "Our hearts have a wonderful capacity to expand and welcome love whether it's from new friendships, or long-lost family, or a new romance. I know, it's tough to do that, at first. I had to let myself be vulnerable, which was the last thing I ever thought I could do again. But if I hadn't done it, I never would've met Zoe. And I love her with all my being. It's not an easy thing, but I promise you, it's definitely worth it."

Able reached out and laid his hand over Morgan's again. "You're one of the bravest people I know and I'm so proud of you, sweetheart. But that tough wall you've built around you, well, maybe it's time to build a door so you can let someone else in."

Morgan chuckled as she wiped her eyes with the back of her hand.

"Ian was an honorable man who loved you with every fiber of his being. And given the kind of man he was, and how much he loved you, I don't think he would want you to be alone the rest of your life. Do you?

"You're right Dad. He wouldn't," she said, sniffing.

"And I think maybe it's time that you opened that door to someone new." Able raised an eyebrow. "And I believe we both know who I'm talking about."

CHAPTER 21

MORGAN DROPPED her costume off at home and took a minute to snuggle Griselda. "I'm sorry. I know I haven't been home much the last few days, but I promise I'll make it up to you. We'll have a beach party or something when this case is solved." The large cat purred, and she was pretty sure the entire house shook. Morgan set Gris on the floor and gave her one long stroke along her spine before adding some treats to her food bowl. "Later, beast. I'm off to catch a killer and grab lunch. Not necessarily in that order."

Morgan climbed into the department issued blue Ford Ranger and made the short drive into town. She parked in front of the station, waved at JJ through the front window, then crossed the street to Dave's Deli. Jerome approached as she slid into her favorite booth.

"Good day to you, Captain. Our specials are a Reuben with fries, chicken salad on croissant with chips, and chili. What'll ya have?"

"You're in an awfully good mood," Morgan observed.

"Weird, right?" Jerome grinned. "It's probably because my boyfriend is coming in from Grand Pere for the festival tonight. We've both been busy lately. Outside of text messaging and video chats, it's been a few weeks since we were actually together."

"That's great, I'm happy for you. And I'll have the Reuben and an iced tea, thanks."

JJ slid onto the bench across from Morgan. "Please make that two Reubens and I'll have a ginger ale," he called out to Jerome who gave him a salute on his way into the kitchen. "I decided to follow the rabbit trail around Geraldine Walker and Fred's tie to the family," JJ said in a low voice. "I dunno. I got a vibe."

A waiter dropped off their drinks and Morgan poured a packet of raw sugar into hers and stirred it with a straw. "You know I respect the vibe. Did you find anything new?"

"I did, actually." JJ sipped his pop. "I uncovered an old adoption record. Fred wasn't Geraldine's son. He was Arthur Jr.'s. It looks like the child was born a month after the crash and immediately put up for adoption."

"Based on what Cal said earlier, that would've made him the male heir Arthur Sr. was pining over. I wonder if the old guy knows he has, well *had*, a grandson?" Jerome came back with their orders. Morgan reached for the ketchup bottle and poured a dollop on the side of her plate. "This is all fascinating, but I'm still not seeing how it ties to our case. What's your vibe say about that?"

JJ had taken a big bite of his sandwich and chewed thoughtfully for a few moments. "My vibe stops there." He shrugged, wiping his fingers on a napkin. "I just thought it was all weird."

"Ed, you really are hilarious!" Tess's laughter reached them as she held the diner door open for the mayor. "You must keep Joan in stitches."

"Well, I've been known to spout more than a few Dad jokes. The cheesier the better, I always say," Ed said as he strolled in.

"Oh, lord," Morgan whispered to JJ.

JJ snickered.

"Captain, Deputy, I didn't expect to see either of you here," Ed said, approaching the officers. "I'm not even taking time for lunch today. Tess and I are getting sandwiches to go so we can keep working for the good people of Bijoux." He looked around the dining room as he said the last part.

"We multi-task. We can eat *and* talk about the case. It's a cop thing. You wouldn't understand."

"What I understand is the lack of information forthcoming from you and how I keep getting it second hand from Connie on the evening news." He frowned. "And it's because of that, I've decided to create a new town position when I get re-elected. Police Liaison." He motioned at Tess. "And I've chosen Tess, here, for the job."

Tess angled her head and smiled at Morgan from the counter. Her perfectly layered dark bob swirled around her like Marlo Thomas in

That Girl. Jerome came out and handed Tess two paper bags. "I have our food," she said. "And I look forward to working with you, Morgan."

Morgan wasn't usually at a loss for words but what she was thinking in this moment, if said out loud, would probably get her fired. "He has absolutely no clue," she said after they left.

"Yeah, I'll keep digging into her," he said.

"It's nice that we're on the same wavelength. I just look at you and you get it," Morgan said with a chuckle. "But seriously. She is so annoying. Bijoux is a small town. The last thing we need is another Connie type interfering between us and the mayor's office."

JJ's phone chimed a message.

"Maggie looking to *not* date two nights in a row?" Morgan asked. She winked at JJ.

"Don't think she hasn't already asked. I told her not tonight. I'm hoping to have a chance to talk to Hannah at some point," he said. "This message is from Doc." He opened his email app and scanned the note. "It's the DNA results for the red hair samples. Sinclaire is not a match, so we can probably cross her off the suspect list." He put the phone down and looked at Morgan. "This is unbelievable."

Morgan frowned. "What's going on?"

"The red hair found at both crime scenes is another match to the Walkers. And it came from a woman." He paid for his food and slid out of the booth. "Guess I know what I'm doing the rest of the afternoon: digging deeper into that one remaining relative of Arthur Walker Sr., Esther Ann."

"While you're doing that, how about you try calling the burner phone randomly. You know, the one that was trying to get hold of Fred? Maybe whoever has it will turn it back on at some point." Morgan slid out of the booth. "I'm going to run over to the carving event. Let me know if you find anything. I'll be back in a bit to help out."

THE REMAINING three competitors were all in the Raven's Nest courtyard, working at their stations for the "big carve' finale. Morgan noted they each had a stack of pumpkins and were creating life-size portraits of Edgar Allan Poe out of them. She observed the carvers for a few moments while they worked. Various groupies hovered close to the fence, watching the contest intently. There was a feeling of tense anticipation in the air, and quite a bit of trash talking between all factions, from what Morgan could hear.

"What time do they finish? And what happens after that?" Morgan asked Ella.

Ella checked the schedule on her tablet. "About thirty minutes. Three p.m. After that, they move their creations to the front of the bookstore so residents and visitors can cast a vote for their favorite. The winner of people's choice contest gets a secondary prize of five hundred dollars. Tess came up with the idea, and we thought it was a great way to get the community engaged. The carvers are excited about it, too. As for the big cash prize, the judges ultimately make that decision."

"And you'll announce the winner at the start of the parade at six?"

"That's the plan." Ella smiled. "In spite of losing Jeff and Fred, this has been one of the smoother competitions we've hosted."

"What do you mean?"

"There's usually a lot more infighting, especially between the different factions of groupies." She considered that for a moment. "Having said that, I suppose most of the ruckus has always been between the Ninja camp and the Phantom gang, so I guess it makes sense things have settled down."

"So, the Ninja and Phantom groupies didn't hang around?"

"Not that I know of. I mean, what's left for them to see at this point?" She looked over at the parking lot where the groupies were set up. "I suppose some of them might still be here, could've just changed teams." She laughed a little. "That happens more often than you'd think."

Which was exactly what Ninja Jeff's three wives had been doing yesterday, except when Morgan scanned today's crowd the sister wives were nowhere to be seen. "Thanks for the scoop, Ella," Morgan said. She walked into the bookstore only to encounter the trio, all wearing their long black robes, and all shouting at Cal.

Cal was standing patiently, holding his hands up in front of him. "Please," he said. "Let's talk about this."

"The time for talking is done," Toody spat. She pulled a pouch out of her robe pocket. "Do you know what this is? It's graveyard dirt. I'm going to curse this place."

Cal dropped his hands. "That's your threat? This place is already cursed. Or at the very least, haunted."

The wives circled him, giving him the stink eye. Toody waved her pouch in his face before turning and leading her sisters to the paranormal section.

"*What* is going on?" Morgan whispered.

He pulled off his glasses and rubbed his eyes. "Apparently, I dissed Ninja Jeff."

"How exactly does one do that?"

"I had some of his merchandise here in the store, some tee shirts and keychains. Little wind-up pumpkins that walked around. I moved them to make room for Vic the Viper's new book of carving patterns." He motioned to the stack near the register. "They just came in today."

"Shhh, they're coming back," Morgan said through the corner of her mouth as she watched the three wives approach once more.

"Where is he?" Nancy asked.

Morgan turned to where Cal had been standing only a few moments ago. "Coward," she said under her breath.

Bridget picked up one of the new books and turned it over. "This picture of Vic is dreamy. Look at how the light captures the snake tattoo wrapped around his head. You'd think it was alive."

Toody snatched the book out of her hand. "Honestly, what is wrong with you?"

Bridget pulled a wand out of her robe pocket and pointed it at the other woman. "Do that again and I'll turn you into a cranky old biddy who looks like a frog." She lowered the wand and smirked. "Oh, hey, no need to. You're already there."

Nancy stepped between the two. "Our fight is with Caleb Joseph, not each other." Standing about six inches taller than Bridget and

Toody, she glared down at them. "It's not like either of you can lay claim to any of Ninja Jeff's fortune, anyway, since I'm the only real wife."

Bridget and Toody stepped back from Nancy, wands raised.

"Oh, for heaven's sake," Morgan said. "All of you, go outside and cool off before I arrest you for disturbing the peace."

Nancy reached over and shoved Vic the Viper's books off the counter. She set a walking toy pumpkin down and blew it a kiss. "That's for you, Jeff." She spun and left the shop, the other wives following close behind.

Cal magically reappeared from one of the storerooms. "Oh, good, they're gone." He picked up the toy and looked it over.

"Like you didn't know." Morgan punched him hard on the arm.

"Ow! What was that for?" he asked, rubbing it.

"For leaving me alone to deal with them. Do something like that again and I'll arrest you."

Cal frowned at her. "On what charge?"

"The same one you always get in trouble for: irritating the police captain."

CHAPTER 22

"WHILE MY SEARCH strings are running on the Walkers, I thought I'd try a different angle with the case," JJ said to Morgan as he spun his chair to face her. "I ran over to where Mayor Ed was handing out his caramel corn—which really is delicious by the way. Cal doesn't stand a chance against it—and got him to sign a warrant to check into the competitor's financials."

Morgan leaned back in her chair. "That's probably the quickest warrant signature on record. I'm betting he asked for your vote at the same time."

JJ chuckled. "That he did. But I remained impartial." He swiveled back to face his monitor. "Most everyone seems on the up and up, usual bills like food and housing. Two stand out, though, with large credit card debt. Vic the Viper and Bobby Rumble."

"How big are we talking?"

"Vic is close to forty grand and Bobby is pushing sixty. That prize money would go a long way for both of them."

Morgan shook her head. "How does someone get that deep in the weeds?"

"From the looks of it, Bobby might have a gambling problem. A lot of his charges are to a horse track in Hamtramck. Vic's receipts just look like day-to-day life stuff—groceries and rent—things like that. Seems he just got really behind. That happened to a cousin of mine once. It's hard to bounce back."

"Sounds like competitive carving only pays if you win, or can cash in on merchandising, which Jeff was doing. Vic just came out with a book. Cal had a display at the shop." Morgan rested her chin on her hands for a moment. "I'd say this definitely pushes Bobby and Vic to the front of the suspect line." She stood and picked up Powerpuff

Buttercup, started tossing her up and down. "We know Jeff and Fred were both favored to win. I wonder who's in the running now?"

"I'm following a chat page on the event. Let me take a look." JJ scanned the comments. "Looks like Bobby Rumble is the trending favorite."

Morgan stopped and faced JJ. "Which means his life could be in danger, if we follow the logic that it's a competitor committing the murders." She grabbed her keys off her desk. "Any luck with the burner phone?"

"Not yet. I have an auto dial app running. It tries to call the number every fifteen minutes. It'll ring to my phone if it comes back on, so I'll have time to pick up the call."

"Excellent." Morgan checked the time. "How is it already five o'clock? Please keep me posted."

JJ saluted. "I always do. And hey, don't forget, we have to be in costume by six for the pre-parade ceremonies. Ed reminded me when he signed the warrant." He lowered his voice a few notes to imitate the mayor, "All town employees are required to dress up."

Morgan made a face. "Right. Thanks for the reminder. I'll swing home and grab my outfit on the way to the judging. Gris will appreciate getting dinner a little early this evening."

A QUICK CAT visit and Morgan was at the Raven's Nest in record time. Cal had outdone himself with the decorations this year. The windows were lined with miniature orange lights, and he'd perched a giant glowing plastic raven on the awning over the doorway. Pumpkins and cornstalks also adorned the front of the shop. He approached her as she opened the driver side door of her truck to get out.

Dressed as Poe himself, Cal bowed and held out his hand. Morgan looked from his proffered hand to his face. She couldn't be sure if his eyes were actually twinkling or if it was just the reflection of the lights. She decided it didn't matter and allowed him to assist her.

"Thank you, kind sir," she said, feeling fancy for a moment.

"Interesting costume," he said, holding her hand up and twirling her. The robe lifted in the back and floated on the air. "Circa 1950s, if I guess correctly. Very Lucille Ball. And you can run in it if you need to. I like it." He smiled.

His compliment was sincere and genuine, and her stomach flip-flopped. He really did have a great smile. *And* he understood her need to run at a moment's notice. *But I can't think about his smile right now. We have to catch a murderer first. Oh, there's always a reason, isn't there?* Her insides were having another argument. *Great.* "Thanks." She stepped back and gestured to the displays. "I see the life-sized carved and stacked Poe pumpkins are set up. It looks like Vic's has the most votes so far."

The pumpkins had been arranged in front of the bookstore with a glass fishbowl next to each for the townsfolk to cast their vote for their favorite. Morgan followed Cal to where they stood. "I voted for Sinclaire's." He stood next to it. "Look like anyone you know?"

"Oh my gosh." Morgan burst out laughing. Sinclaire had obviously used Cal for a model. "Did you pose for that?"

"I did not. When I asked her about it, she blushed and acted embarrassed, so I let it go."

"Well, it looks like she might have a crush on you."

Cal grinned. "She's a sweetheart. But I'm not interested."

"Met someone on that dating app already, did you?"

Before he could reply, Ella yelled, "Captain Morgan! We need your help!"

Both Morgan and Cal rushed over to where Ella was standing just outside the courtyard fence. Morgan didn't need to ask what was wrong. Sinclaire Wild and Vic the Viper were squared off like they were ready to do battle. "What the hell?" Morgan asked.

Neither competitor looked at her, kept their eyes trained on the other. "Vic was tampering with the votes. It's why he's ahead right now."

"Maybe I just have the best carving. Besides, you can't prove anything."

The Siamese cat hissed from his carrier on Sinclaire's work bench. "See? Hebrides has a sixth sense for evil. He knows you're lying," she accused.

"You two stand down," Morgan said. "Vic, go grab a seat at your bench. I'll talk to you in a moment." She faced Sinclaire. "What are you thinking? He's at least twice your size."

"I don't care. It isn't right."

Okay, that Morgan could understand. She believed in standing up against injustice, too. It's one of the reasons she was a cop.

"If it helps, those votes don't matter in the grand scheme of things," Ella said as she approached the two women. "Like I mentioned earlier to the captain, we're only using them for the People's Choice award. The judges decide who wins the big prize money."

Sinclaire clenched and unclenched her jaw. "Anything else?" She asked Morgan.

Morgan shook her head and shifted her focus to Vic. She waved him over. "What the hell, Vic? You do good work. Do you really need to cheat to win?"

He shrugged. "Maybe I do, maybe I don't." He leaned in and whispered, "But I do know who the pumpkin killer is."

She crossed her arms. "And who would that be?"

"Bobby Rumble. I heard him bragging about how he was taking out the competition, one by one." He nodded over at Bobby who was on the other side of the fence, signing autographs for his groupies. "Just look at him. Shady."

Morgan followed Vic's gaze. Bobby looked relaxed and happy. "I know you're up to your eyeballs in debt, Vic. Where were you early Thursday morning? Before the pumpkin picking."

Vic jutted his chin out. "A gentleman never divulges such things."

"I can understand that," Cal said from behind Morgan.

"I heard you approaching this time," she said to Cal over her shoulder. "Just so you know, you're not as stealthy as you think you are."

"Challenge accepted," he said with a wink.

Morgan raised an eyebrow, and returned her full attention to Vic. She wasn't opposed to flirting, but not when questioning a potential suspect. "If you have an alibi, Vic, I need to hear it now."

He looked down, kicked at some grass, then met Morgan's eyes. "Bridget. I was with Bridget."

"Ninja Jeff's wife Bridget?" Cal asked. "Wow."

"Well, it's not like she's actually his wife since he was already married to Nancy. Besides, she told me she was leaving him; she was tired of all his lies."

"You do know I'm going to have to talk to her, to corroborate your story," Morgan said.

"Yeah, I know." He sighed and Morgan thought he was actually tearing up a bit. "I hope she'll forgive me for telling you. I really like her."

Morgan left Vic where he was standing, walked around the gate, and approached Bobby Rumble and his groupies. "Seems you're popular today."

"Please. I'm always popular. Just ask them." He waved his arm at the folks gathered around him and they cheered. The other sets of groupies booed.

"More popular with some than others," Morgan observed. She scanned the gathering, noticed the wives were back, skulking through the crowd. "Can we talk privately for a moment?"

"Whatever you need to say to me, you can say in front of my fans."

"I don't think so."

"You'll have to. I have nothing to hide and I'm not moving from here until it's time to announce the winner. These are my people." He raised both arms up in the air and his followers cheered again.

"All right. It's possible you could be in danger, so please be careful."

Bobby's face went blank. "What? What do you mean?"

"Both Ninja Jeff and Phantom Fred were favored to win. Since they're gone, you're the new favorite. Just be aware of your surroundings, okay?"

His groupies circled around him. "We'll keep you safe, Rumble. You can count on us."

"This doesn't feel safe. This feels claustrophobic," Bobby said, his eyes darting back and forth..

They started chanting, "Rumble is the one! Rumble is the one!"

Morgan shook her head and went to talk to Bridget.

CHAPTER 23

"BRIDGET? A WORD, PLEASE."

Bridget lifted her chin. "I have nothing to say to you."

Toody and Nancy joined the conversation. "You can't arrest us for putting a curse on Caleb Joseph. The man deserved it," Nancy said.

"Curse away. That's not why I'm here." Morgan focused on Bridget. "Vic the Viper says he was with you Thursday morning, at the time of Jeff's murder. Can you verify his claim?"

Nancy took a step toward Bridget, her eyes narrowed. "What did you do?"

Bridget squared her shoulders. "I like him. He treats me well and, as far as I can tell, hasn't married a bunch of groupies. Not at the same time, at least."

"You sully the name of our Ninja," Toody said.

Bridget crossed her arms over chest and turned her back on her sister wives. "It's true," she said to Morgan. "I met up with Vic on Wednesday evening and left his room Thursday morning. Around seven, I think."

"And neither of you noticed she was missing?" Morgan asked Nancy and Toody.

"We have our own tents. I suppose she could have sneaked out," Nancy said. She glared at the other woman. "This is a betrayal, Bridget!"

"To hell with the *Ninja*. And to hell with both of you," Bridget shouted back, swinging around to confront the two women. "I'm outta here." She pulled off her robe, shoved it at Nancy, and marched off toward Vic's groupies.

Nancy and Toody looked like they were ready to run her down.

Possibly with a large automobile. "Don't do anything stupid," Morgan warned.

"Not a chance," Nancy said, relaxing. "She's not worth the trouble."

"Hey, Captain!"

Morgan turned to see JJ heading toward her. He was dressed as the Tin Man, his face painted silver, and carrying an axe with a sign that read, *Have you seen my heart*? He also had his laptop under his arm.

"Nice costume. That sign addressed to anyone in particular?" She couldn't be certain but was pretty sure he blushed under his silvery makeup. "What's up?"

"Let's talk inside. I've discovered something we should go over."

They entered the bookstore and Morgan called out to Cal, "We're going to use one of your small meeting rooms."

He shot her a thumbs up. *Weird*. He wasn't a 'thumbs up' kind of guy.

Morgan closed the door. "What do you have, JJ?"

"Besides tracing the carvers, I've also been running those concurrent search strings on the Walkers," JJ said. He opened his laptop and showed Morgan the screen where he'd listed his talking points. He started counting off on his fingers. "Now, we already know that David Walker, the founder, left the company to Arthur Walker Sr. We also know that Arthur Sr. had one daughter and one son. Geraldine Walker and Arthur Walker Jr. And we know that Geraldine had a daughter and Jr. had a son, who was adopted out. The son, as we know, is our victim, Phantom Fred."

"Good summary. How about Fred's birth mom?" Morgan asked. "Were you able to find her or any other next of kin on that side of the family?"

JJ shook his head. "I located her data through the adoption records, but she passed last year, no close family. Fred was never actually adopted, so no family there, either. He spent his childhood in and out of foster homes."

"Wow, that had to be a horrible way to grow up." Morgan leaned back in her chair and crossed her ankles. "How about Geraldine's daughter? Is she still around?"

"Near as I can tell, yes, she is. I finally located her birth certificate. It confirmed the name Cal shared from the autobiography, Esther Ann Walker. Esther Ann would be thirty-five years old now."

Cal walked in carrying a large book. "I have a working theory on your case," he said.

"What makes you think we're talking about the case? For all you know, we could be going over JJ's inability to understand what a date is," Morgan offered. "Not the investigation."

"Yeah, we need to work on that." Cal laughed, then grew serious. "But you can't tell me you're not investigating." He motioned with his hand. "Look how you're huddled in here." He grabbed a chair and positioned it across from them.

Morgan uncrossed her ankles and sat up. "Welcome to the huddle," she said. "All right. What's your working theory?" He might be a giant pain, but his ideas weren't always horrible. There was something compelling about the way he could put pieces together.

Cal held the book up he'd brought in with him, a copy of Alan Walker Sr.'s autobiography.

"And?" Morgan asked.

"*And*, there's a family tree in the back. The old man is very proud of his heritage, traces it all the way back to the Mayflower."

Morgan let out a long sigh. "What's your point, Cal? We're burning time here."

He laid the book on the table, opened to the chart, and pointed at one section. "David Walker's wife's name was Esther."

JJ and Morgan both stared at him. "The great-granddaughter was named after her. So what?" Morgan said.

"I didn't finish. Here's the *piece de resistance*—The original Esther's last name was Clooney."

Morgan leaned forward and studied the family tree, her eyes narrowed on the information before her. "And Tess is an old nickname for Esther." She looked up. "Tess Clooney is Esther Ann Walker."

"That's my theory, too," Cal said. "Or, at the very least, a cousin of some sort."

"Too coincidental," JJ said. "Captain doesn't believe in coincidences."

"I do not. However, if the crime *is* associated with the Walkers, it still doesn't explain Jeff Malone's death," Morgan said. "Unless it really was a simple case of mistaken identity. Wrong place, wrong time."

"I think you're right, given how much they resembled each other," Cal said.

"Whew," JJ said. "At least that means we should only have one killer this time around. And it's likely a relative of the Walkers."

"Tess Clooney. She's the missing piece," Morgan said.

"According to this book, if she is Esther Ann, she's also the sole heir to the Walker fortune. If you go with money as the driving factor, well, she doesn't need it," Cal said.

"Motivation comes from different places for different people." Morgan pushed up from her chair. "I'm going to go have a chat with our possibly soon to be Police Liaison."

CHAPTER 21

MORGAN STRODE out of the bookstore to the front, where the judges were getting ready to announce the Pumpkins and Poe winner. It was dusk and a local band was playing in the town square across the street, signaling the start of the pre-parade festivities. Morgan couldn't believe her eyes at the trio—Doc Pete the Veterinarian on guitar, Beau Cornet, the butcher, on drums, and Mr. Dominic on clarinet. The elderly man wielded his musical instrument as deftly as he did this cane. Surprisingly, they were pretty good. Someone had started a bonfire near the band and the scent of burning wood filtered through the air.

"Tess. A word please?"

Tess looked up, irritation etched on her face. "We're busy. Whatever it is, it'll have to wait."

"We're ready to start filming the announcement of the results," Ella said from behind Tess. "Do you mind holding off for a few, Captain? It won't take long."

Morgan sighed and stepped aside. Tess wasn't going anywhere. "Go ahead."

A small dais had been constructed near the pumpkin display. Sal climbed the two short steps to the top and looked out over the crowd. Ella handed him a wireless microphone. "Welcome to the culmination of our three-day event and the crowning of the next *Astounding Pumpkins* winner. Would the three remaining contestants please step forward and stand by your creations?"

Sinclaire, Vic, and Bobby all took their places. Morgan noted Sinclaire seemed nervous, but Vic and Bobby didn't seem phased at all.

"The winner of the People's Choice goes to," Sal paused for dramatic effect, "Sinclaire Wild!"

"Oh my gosh!" she shouted, running over to Sal and giving him a big hug. She turned to the crowd. "Thank you!"

Sal stepped down and Tess took over his spot. "And now, it's time to announce the winner of the fifty-thousand-dollar prize!"

The crowd cheered.

"And the overall winner is—" At that moment, Tess's cell phone rang. She pulled it out of her cross-body purse and hit the 'cancel' button. "Sorry. Awkward," she joked, and chuckles rippled through the crowd. "Back to the business at hand. And the winner is—Vic the Viper! Vic, come and get your check!"

Ricky Rock n' Roll appeared, carrying one of those giant checks you see on game shows. The crowd clapped and cheered, and the band started playing again. Audrey, Mr. Dominic's girlfriend, was standing in front of them, swaying and waving a lighter in the air.

"Where do you even cash a check that big?" Morgan wondered aloud.

"You don't. That's for show," Cal said from behind her. "He'll get a regular check, too."

She grinned at him. "Still didn't scare me."

"I have something that might," JJ whispered from where he stood next to Cal. "Okay, it's not scary, but that call Tess just got? That was me, calling the burner phone."

"How can you be sure?"

He held up his phone. "The app I'm using routed the call back to me when her phone rang. She shut it off at exactly the same time the call ended. The app also activated a GPS tracker. You can see, the phone is right here." He pointed at the green dot on the screen. It was about ten feet away from their current position.

"That's an invasion of privacy. Please tell me that program is limited to police use?" Cal said.

"Well, yeah, of course it's limited to law enforcement. But that doesn't mean people don't find ways around it," JJ replied. "Like anything else out there, if someone wants something badly enough, they'll figure out how to get it."

"Let's go talk to Tess," Morgan said, "and find out what she wanted so badly that she kept trying to meet with Fred."

As the trio approached her, Tess took a step forward and planted her hands on her hips. "Now what is so important?" she asked Morgan.

"That burner phone in your purse," Morgan said. She held out her hand. "May I see it?"

"I have no idea what you're talking about."

JJ dialed it and it pinged. "That phone right there," he said.

Tess glanced around her.

"If you're thinking about running, you won't get far." Morgan held up a foot. "I have my running boots on and you're wearing heels. How about we go inside and chat?"

They entered the bookstore and Morgan directed a reluctant Tess to a meeting room. "Have a seat, please."

"What's Cal doing here? He's not a cop," Tess said. She flashed him a toothy smile. "Unless you brought him along as eye candy. That, I'm good with."

Cal sat down and tilted his head at her, his gaze narrowing. "You might want to hold that thought." He opened the autobiography to a photo of Esther Ann as a young girl and pushed the book to the center of the table.

Tess stopped smiling.

Morgan leaned in and scanned the photo. "That's a lot of red hair. Even though you've changed your name and you're older now, my bet is you'll be a DNA match for both the Walkers and the red hair we found at both of the murder scenes. And we'll most likely find trace evidence of your DNA on the robe you dressed Sinclaire in after you knocked her out at Gourds Galore."

"That's ridiculous," Tess said. She flipped her brunette mane. "Does this look like a dye job?"

"Testing will show us that, too."

Tess sat back and crossed her arms and legs. "I'm not giving up my DNA. You'll have to get a warrant."

"No problem. JJ, I saw Ed out on the square with the band. How about you go get his signature on a release?"

"I'm on it," JJ said and hurried out of the room.

Tess stared at Morgan, her expression like that of an ace poker player.

She's calm under pressure; I'll give her that. "You *are* Geraldine's daughter," Morgan said. She glanced down at the photo spread in the book. "You look just like her. I am sorry for your loss. My mom passed a few years back, too. I understand how hard it can be."

"I know you're just trying to buddy up to me. Find common ground. It won't work, Captain." She brushed at an imaginary piece of lint. "If you don't mind, I'd like to get back to the festival now."

"Arthur Sr. found out about Fred, didn't he? Hired a private investigator?"

"Please, nothing that dramatic. Some second cousin twice removed found a match to Fred on *Find My Ancestors*. Apparently, Fred was looking for his birth family."

"I imagine it's challenging being the only heir to an old man's fortune when the old man doesn't think you're good enough for the legacy." Morgan's eyes met hers and she knew she'd touched a nerve. Tess's eyes flashed with rage. "And that's why you killed him. You didn't want to share."

Tess looked up at the ceiling, her jaw ticking. "He made my mother miserable," she spat out. "To hell with *grandpa* and his long-lost *grandson*. I've put up with the old man's BS my entire life about how I wasn't good enough because I wasn't a boy. My mother was hospitalized twice for attempted suicide before she turned twenty-one. She married that playboy just to get away from dear old Dad. Of course, Baron Touissant, the man who sired me, was a useless piece of nihilistic French trash, who broke Mom's heart. Everything I did, I did for her. To protect *her* legacy." She jumped up from her chair, slammed her fist on the table. "I deserve the money if for no other reason than that."

Morgan realized she'd been holding her breath and let it out. "But why kill Jeff? What's with that note, *Nevermore*?"

Tess started pacing in the small room. "I only had photos of Fred." She stopped and looked at all of them. "I thought Jeff was Fred. Though after hearing about all of the Ninja's exploits this weekend, I'd say the jerk deserved it." She screwed up her mouth. "Three wives.

Who even does that? And *Nevermore*? Because all this patriarchal nonsense ends with me."

Morgan stood, turned Tess around. She read Tess her rights as she pulled a pair of handcuffs out of the top of her boot and secured the other woman's hands.

"So that's where you carry everything," Cal said. "I always wondered."

"A good pair of boots will always serve you well."

JJ returned with the signed warrant for the DNA test, and took in the scene. "Okay, then. Looks like the mystery is solved."

"Please have Doc run those DNA tests right away to confirm the evidence."

"C'mon, Tess. I'll get you swabbed and set up in the cell until we can transfer you to county tomorrow."

"I want to talk to my attorney."

"You can do that once we get you settled," JJ said.

"Thanks, JJ," Morgan said. "See you back here in a bit?"

"Maybe. I want to try to talk to Hannah first," he called over his shoulder as he exited the room. "Wish me luck."

Cal stood and crooked his elbow. "You deserve a break after the last few days. Join me for the festivities?"

"Wouldn't miss it." Morgan smiled and linked arms with him. "I'm starving," Morgan said as they walked out onto the street and into the holiday crowd. Everyone was wearing costumes and the kids were trick or treating at the various shops and stores along Main Street. "How about we hit Frankie's first?"

"Sounds good to me."

They crossed the street and walked the couple of blocks down to the Perch Mouth. The patio area was packed, but they were able to find a couple of stools at the bar. Frankie was there, dressed like a banshee in a gray gauzy robe, white face paint, black circles around her eyes, and she'd teased her short hair into a mohawk and adorned it with fake cobwebs. "That's quite a costume," Morgan remarked. "Did you get it from Zoe?"

Frankie laughed. "I did! She has the best selection and I'm grateful she shares with me."

"Well, you *are* like another daughter to them."

"I like to think so." Frankie grinned. "Now, what can I get you two? The usual?"

"Works for me," Cal said.

Morgan nodded. Cal's phone pinged and he checked the message. She watched his face grow serious. "Is everything all right?"

"Um, yeah. Yes." His eyes met hers. "It's my agent. She's negotiated a seven-figure deal for my Philip McDonald mystery series, including TV rights."

"Oh my gosh! That's amazing!" Morgan said. "Wait, did you say *seven* figures? As in a million?"

"And then some."

"You know what this means, don't you?" Morgan asked. "It means you're paying tonight. For everything. Including the games."

Frankie placed Morgan's usual stout, along with Cal's hard cider, on the bar in front of them. "Cal, you look like you've seen, well, me. Are you okay?" she asked.

"He just found out he's getting a million dollars for his new book series and he's in shock," Morgan explained. "Oh, and he's paying for all my stuff tonight."

Cal looked at the two women. "This means I can't be mayor. I have a tight deadline to turn the first book around. I can't work on this new series, run the bookstore, and the town." He frowned. "I have to withdraw from the race."

"You can't!" Frankie all but shouted, drawing the attention of some of the patrons. She lowered her voice. "We need you in there, fighting the good fight for us merchants."

"You should do it, Frankie," Morgan said. "Take his place on the ballot. Everyone knows you."

"No way that'll work," Frankie said. "I have this place to run."

Morgan made a face at her friend. "Please. You have plenty of good help. If you don't run, Ed will get reelected. Do you want to have to deal with him for the next two years hounding you about changing the paint color of your sign or anything else he thinks of? Or how about Mr. Dominic? Do you want him hanging around outside the Perch Mouth, yelling at people not to cut the line?"

Frankie sighed. "I hear you. You make a strong argument. But the election is in three days. There's no time to get a campaign going."

"I'll help," Cal said. "You jump in, and I'll work on getting the word out."

Morgan squeezed Frankie's hand. "You got this."

Frankie looked from Cal to Morgan. "I can't believe I'm doing this, but okay, okay." A server brought their fried perch, slaw, and fries. "Now eat. I'm going to go distract myself with work before I change my mind."

CHAPTER 25

WITHIN THE SHORT span of Saturday to Monday, the weather had shifted noticeably. The air was cooler, and the crisp winds had shaken most of the trees bare, signaling the coming winter. Shop owners were in the process of taking down their Halloween decorations to make room for Thanksgiving.

Morgan sat at her desk, sipping her coffee, and contemplating how more than the weather was shifting. She felt herself changing. Softening where she'd been hard. Opening where she'd been closed. Despite the spate of murders since she'd come home, her time in Bijoux had definitely been good for her. Or so she hoped.

There was something about moving into colder days and nights that always turned her inward. She shook off the reverie. "Hey, JJ. Do you need any help with Tess?" JJ was in the back, readying the woman for transport to the Odawa County jail. Arnie Hart, the sheriff and Morgan's uncle, had been notified and was expecting the prisoner.

"Thanks, but I'm good."

The bell on the front door to the station chimed as Hannah walked in, carrying what looked like a box of treats. Morgan stood and greeted her at the counter with a smile. "Hey, Hannah. I see you survived the festival."

Hannah laughed. "It was touch and go there for a bit. I was lucky to have Paul to help out. I was swamped with sales and orders."

"That doesn't sound like a bad thing." Morgan followed Hannah's gaze to where it skimmed over JJ. *Now that's yearning if I ever saw it.* "How is Paul, by the way?"

"Oh, he's fine." Hannah refocused on Morgan. "He left yesterday morning and headed to the U.P. to meet his fiancée for a camping trip. Superior State Park."

"Fiancée, you say?" Morgan glanced back at JJ who suddenly dropped his keys. *These two. I might have to step in here.* "I didn't realize he was engaged."

"Yeah, has been for a while. I haven't met her yet, but he's supposed to bring her next time he comes to Bijoux. Anyway, I brought these." She opened the magenta box to display the half dozen cupcakes inside.

Morgan picked one up and inhaled the deep chocolate aroma. "These smell amazing. I bet they taste even better." She took a small bite and moaned. "So, so good, Hannah. Thank you for bringing them by. It's always appreciated."

"Actually," Hannah began, "I was thinking they'd be good for a road trip."

JJ walked Tess up to the counter, transfer paperwork in hand. "I'm ready to go, Captain."

"Are those chocolate?" Tess asked, peering into the box. "I need some good chocolate. You guys have a terrible jail menu. My attorney will be addressing that, by the way."

Hannah looked at JJ. "If it's all right with you, I thought I might ride along. Maybe we could have that talk." She shrugged, like it didn't matter either way. "Maybe we can grab lunch after dropping Tess off?"

Morgan knew Hannah was trying to be noncommittal, but she could see the fear of rejection in her eyes.

JJ started to grin, then tamped it down to a casual nod. "Yeah. Sure. Sounds good."

Morgan pushed the box of cupcakes at JJ, but not before grabbing a second one. "Don't forget these."

THE FOLLOWING DAY, Election Day, saw the three candidates—the incumbent Ed Peltier, Mr. Dominic, and Frankie Whitaker—all sitting outside town hall surrounded by their fans. Ed's group held up signs supporting Ed's campaign mandate—*Clean up Bijoux* and *Tourist Dollars are at Stake*. Mr. Dominic's small faction who loved perch dinners and hated line cutters were all waving canes in the air; and Frankie's team, who seemed the most laid back of the bunch, were busy passing out flyers advertising specials at the bar.

The sun was low on the horizon, voting was over, and the election board, headed up by Morgan's dad Able, was tallying votes. Bijoux wasn't a big town, so they'd have the results within the hour.

"It's like the pumpkin groupies all over again," Morgan muttered to herself as she joined Frankie. "It looks like Cal did a pretty good job of pivoting voters away from his camp and over to yours," she said to her friend.

Frankie grabbed Morgan's arm and pulled her down. She whispered into Morgan's ear, "What am I going to do if I win this thing?"

Morgan squatted next to Frankie's chair. "Oh, for heaven's sake. You're a successful and accomplished business owner. You'll run the town and do a better job of it than Ed ever hoped to. Remember when you were eighth grade class president? You managed to get all the kids to come together on that one key issue of adding chocolate chip cookies to the lunch dessert menu."

"That's because the only other dessert was apple sauce."

"Well, you galvanized everyone, and won. That's exactly what we need in Bijoux."

Frankie frowned. "These aren't kids."

"No, but a lot of them certainly act like it."

Frankie burst out laughing. "You're not lying."

"Is it my shirt?" Cal asked as he joined Morgan and Frankie. He spun around. "Purple is the new black, so I don't see what's so funny about it."

"Holy crap, not everything is about you," Morgan said. "But I like the shirt. It's a good color on you."

Cal grinned. "Why, thank you, Captain."

"May I have your attention, please?" Able stood on the town hall steps, a sheet of paper in his hands. "We have our count and are ready to announce a winner."

Connie pushed her way through the crowd, mike held out and camera rolling to her right.

"And our next mayor is—Frankie Whitaker!"

Frankie's jaw dropped.

"You did it!" Morgan said.

"I did it?"

"You won!" Cal added.

"Oh my God, I won!"

Morgan wrapped her arms around her friend and hugged her close.

Connie rushed up to Frankie and shoved the microphone at her face. "Would you like to make a statement, Madam Mayor-elect?"

"Wow. Just wow. Thank you, all, for your vote of confidence. I promise to do my best for Bijoux. And I promise to have a better acceptance speech planned for my swearing in."

The crowd applauded and cheered. Mr. Dominic walked over to congratulate Frankie. "Well, I do like your perch. I can see that may have tipped the scales in your favor. But if you need me to deal with line cutters, you let me know."

"Thanks, I'll do that, Mr. Dominic."

Ed approached with his wife, Joan; his face looked white and pale.

He hesitated and with a jab from his wife's elbow, he held out his hand to Frankie. "We, uh, we haven't always seen eye to eye, but I'll be around if I can help with anything."

"I appreciate that, Ed." Frankie shook his hand.

"Congratulations Frankie, all the best," Joan said. She was all smiles. Morgan couldn't blame her; she was probably relieved this was over and she could go back to tending her prize-winning roses.

Ed nodded.

"Come along dear," his wife said. "Let's go home."

"Home. Yes."

They turned and made their way down Main Street as their supporters surrounded them with words of condolences.

"He looks like he's just been to his own funeral," Cal said.

"Well, if it's a funeral, Joan certainly isn't mourning. She looks happy the mayor is dead and she can have her husband Ed back."

"And hopefully he'll be nicer to everyone," Frankie said. "Cal, how about you grab that cooler from behind my chair and we celebrate?"

MORGAN SAT WITH HER FRIENDS, talking about all the things Frankie hoped to do for Bijoux and about Cal's new book series. Her phone pinged a message from Liz. *We have a firm date for the trial. November 15th. Looking forward to seeing you. Let's put this scum bag where he belongs, behind bars. Along with our former captain. BTW, I'm so excited for Frankie. She texted me. Going to try to come over for a visit next weekend.*

"Everything okay?" Cal asked.

"It's Liz. The trial for Wheat starts on the 15th. I'll need to be in Detroit on the 14th to prep."

"I'm going with you."

"What? Why? You don't need to do that."

"I know I don't." He ran a hand through his dark hair. "You can call it research for my book if that makes you feel less itchy. But the truth is, I want to be there for you."

"Let him go with you, Morgan," Frankie urged. "You know he has your back."

Morgan's eyes met Cal's and she held his gaze for a few moments. *You don't have to do everything alone anymore.* That was true. She had people around who cared about her. Dad and Zoe were right. It was time to let someone else in. Maybe that someone was Caleb Joseph. She smiled. "I do know that." She held up her drink and tilted it toward Cal. "Just like I have his."

A NOTE FROM TERI BARNETT

I hope you enjoyed ***Pumpkins are Murder***, Bijoux Mystery Series: Book 4.

If you'd like to leave a review, which I'd greatly appreciate, please visit Amazon.com.

I love to hear from readers! You can contact me through my website at www.teribarnett.com. While you're there, please go ahead and subscribe to my newsletter so you can stay up to date on new releases, special offers, and giveaways.

And, for a special holiday treat, keep reading for a Sneak Peek of ***Mistletoe is Murder***, Bijoux Mystery Series: Book 5!

Sneak Peek

MISTLETOE IS MURDER

Bijoux Mystery Series: Book 5

"I did it!" Caleb Joseph exclaimed as he strode into the Perch Mouth Bar and Grille, an old shotgun style bar with lakeside charm. It was a sunny Saturday afternoon in mid-December and a rush of cold air came through the door with him. He peeled off his black nylon winter coat, waved at a couple of other customers, and dropped onto a stool next to Morgan Hart, Bijoux, Michigan's police captain.

"Did you finally get that cat you've been wanting?" Morgan asked, smiling. Cal was a former University of Michigan professor, best-selling author, and owner of the town's bookstore, the Raven's Nest. He was also her good friend, something Morgan had been pondering quite a bit lately. After five years, her husband, Ian's, murder was finally solved, the killer was behind bars, and Morgan could take a breath. While she'd always hold Ian close, she'd begun to think it might be time to open her heart again and make room for someone new. And maybe Cal was that someone…

"I do still need to do that," Cal said thoughtfully, then added, "But no, the big news is I bought the old Lawrence place. That red brick two-story house right on Lake Michigan, just down the road from the Firefly Bed and Breakfast."

Francine 'Frankie' Whitaker, proprietor of the Perch Mouth, one of Morgan's best friends since childhood, and Bijoux's mayor-elect, poured a stout for Morgan and Cal's usual cherry hard cider. "I know it well and I had no idea you were even looking at it," Frankie said, setting their drinks down on the bar. "I heard it was condemned."

"I heard there were raccoons living in it." Morgan playfully nudged Cal with her elbow. "I get that you have all that money now from the major TV deal for your detective mystery series but why on earth would you buy a raccoon house?"

Cal scrubbed a hand over his day-old beard and adjusted his black horned rim glasses on his nose. "There are no raccoons. At least I haven't seen any. Now I'll have to get the chimneys checked." He rested his elbows on the oak and linoleum counter and sipped his cider. "I thought you'd both be excited for me, not pick at all the things that are wrong about my new home."

"Oh, please. Suggesting you may have a furry infestation isn't being critical," Morgan said. "That house has been empty for what? Maybe twenty years? It's bound to have critters scurrying about." Morgan took a sip of her beer. *Coffee chocolate goodness.* "So, I guess this means you're moving out of the apartment over the bookstore?"

"Eventually. After the Lawrence family moved east in the nineties, they used the house for summer vacations for several years. Then, for whatever reason, they all just stopped coming. The basement, attic, and garage are stacked full of boxes. Apparently, no one in the family thought it was worth a trip back here to retrieve any of it, so it all came along with the sale. My plan is to get a good portion of the downstairs cleaned up and repaired right away, have the contractor ready to start on Monday." He grinned at Morgan and Frankie. "Then I'm throwing a big Christmas Eve bash to celebrate and you're both invited."

"Oooh, sounds fun," Frankie said. "Can I bring a date?"

"Liz is always welcome," Cal said with a smile.

Liz Shore was Morgan's partner from when she worked homicide in Detroit. When Liz came to town for Morgan's dad's wedding, she and Frankie connected, and were now in a long-distance relationship.

"I'm in. Especially if you're going to have raccoon butlers wearing tiny red bowties and Santa hats," Morgan said. "Wouldn't that be something?"

Cal laughed. "I can absolutely promise you won't see that." He leaned in and whispered, "What I can't promise, though, is you won't see a ghost. According to historical records, my new house was a stop on the rum runner pirate trail between Canada and Chicago during prohibition. Supposedly more than one met their demise on the property." He downed the rest of his drink. "It'll be interesting to see what we discover in the renovation."

"Well, as you know, I don't believe in ghosts," Morgan whispered back. "But I'm sure it will be a one-of-a-kind Christmas party."

I hope you enjoyed this sneak peek of
Mistletoe is Murder
Bijoux Mystery Series: Book 5

Visit Amazon.com to purchase your copy!

ABOUT THE AUTHOR

Teri Barnett is the author of the Bijoux Mystery Series and the upcoming Lac Voo Mystery Series as well as numerous non-fiction books about Reiki. In a past life, she also wrote historical time-travel/paranormal romance (check out her Oracle Dreams Trilogy).

In addition to writing, Teri is an award-winning artist and nationally recognized commercial interior designer who brings a lifetime of learning and exploration to her writing and workshops. Born and raised in Michigan, Teri currently resides in Indiana where she writes books, does cool art, crochets too many shawls and afghans, and hangs out with Black Cat Lou, her bossy black cat. Though not a Maine Coon, BCL *is* the inspiration for Morgan's rescue cat, Griselda, who makes her debut in Book 2, Mystics are Murder.

When Teri isn't busy working on her next book or redesigning the world, you can find her doing the artist thing in her studio (painting or designing book covers), tromping through the forest, hanging with her kids and grandbabies, or riding through the corn tunnels of Indiana on her motorcycle.

You can visit Teri online at www.teribarnett.com to learn more about her books, contact her, and/or subscribe to her newsletter. Want to follow Lou's antics? You can find her on Insta @TheBlackCatLou.

ALSO BY TERI BARNETT

BIJOUX MYSTERY SERIES

Romance is Murder: Bijoux Mystery Series Book 1

A dead diva, a rotten romance, and a town full of nosy neighbors...

Morgan Hart is home. A former homicide detective in Detroit, Morgan is back in her old hometown of Bijoux, Michigan to take over the reins of Sheriff from her dad, Able. The town has undergone quite a transformation since she lived here with new, kitschy shops along Main Street and a burgeoning tourist trade. Even the iconic pink Firefly Bed & Breakfast has jumped on the bandwagon and is hosting a romance writers' convention with some of the biggest names in the 'happily ever after' biz.

Morgan hopes to ease into her new job, new cottage, and new life – after all, Bijoux hasn't had a murder in a hundred years. But all of Morgan's plans go up in smoke when the biggest diva of the romance world is found dead.

As Morgan and her deputy, JJ Jones, begin their investigation, the townspeople have no qualms about telling her how to do her job, including Caleb Joseph, owner of the local bookstore who is far too nosy (and attractive) for Morgan's comfort.

With a murder to solve and the town in turmoil, Morgan will have to rely on her big city cop skills to catch a killer harboring a hate for happy endings.

Mystics are Murder: Bijoux Mystery Series Book 2

What do you do when your star murder witness only speaks 'Meow?'

Who could predict it would happen again? Morgan Hart didn't expect her first day as police captain of Bijoux, Michigan, the sleepy lakeside town where she grew up, would include a murder, even though that's just what happened. But with the killer behind bars, Morgan can take a breath and start painting her cozy cottage.

Or so she hopes.

When a fortune-telling mystic is found dead at Bijoux's Walk into the Light Psychic Gathering, Morgan and her deputy, JJ Jones, are called in to investigate. The trouble is Morgan's only witness is Griselda, a black cat with blood on her paws.

While every psychic in town claims to know what the cat 'knows,' Morgan relies on her own instincts to sniff out the suspects while dodging her conflicting feelings for local bookshop owner and town hunk, Caleb Joseph. And with her dad, Able's, upcoming wedding to Zoe Buffet, Bijoux's most famous clairvoyant and coffee cake queen, Morgan is under the gun to figure out which mystic is the murderer before the couple says I do.

Cupcakes are Murder: Bijoux Mystery Series Book 3

A cupcake conundrum, a culinary queen on the edge, and a cold-case killer on the loose...

Morgan Hart is settling into her job as police captain of Bijoux, the quaint and quirky tourist town nestled on the Lake Michigan shoreline. Murders have been solved, kittens have been rescued, and progress has been made in the renovation of her cozy cottage by the beach. Despite her grief and ongoing frustration over her husband's unsolved murder six years ago, Morgan hopes an overdue break in the case will finally lead to justice, even if it means exposing a betrayal that could leave her reeling.

Meanwhile, Morgan needs to keep a sharp eye on the upcoming Baker's Dozen Hometown Cupcake Bake-off and TV special hosted by British baking superstar Sassy McComas, aka The Queen of Cupcakes. Rumor has it, Queen Sass is secretly searching for a fresh face to host a new TV show and the competitors vying for the top spot include Bijoux's own pastry princess, Hannah Bellamy.

But when one of the top challengers in the Cupcake Bake-off turns up dead,

Morgan has to sift through the evidence and stop the killer before they strike again and threaten to topple Queen Sass from her throne.

Pumpkins are Murder: Bijoux Mystery Series Book 4

A dead carver, dueling witches, and more tricks than treats...

Bijoux, Michigan is serious about Halloween.

Known as the most haunted town on the Lake Michigan shoreline, Bijoux hosts the annual Pumpkins and Poe Festival—the town's annual homage to Edgar Allan Poe and all things spooky. Pumpkin carvers from around the country flock to Bijoux, slicing and dicing their way into Halloween history. But when one of the carvers turns up dead with a jack-o-lantern on their head and a note with the word Nevermore scrawled in orange ink pinned to their apron, police captain Morgan Hart is called in to investigate.

After solving multiple murders at three previous Bijoux events, the beleaguered police captain steps into the fray once again, along with her down-in-the-dumps deputy, JJ Jones, recently ditched by his girlfriend, local cupcake maven, Hannah Bellamy. Meanwhile, Morgan's own "weak and weary" heart keeps getting tested by Caleb Joseph, owner of the Raven's Nest bookstore. The too-hot-for-his-own-good former Gothic Lit professor has made a hobby out of snooping around Morgan's cases.

It's up to Morgan to thwart various Halloween high-jinks around Bijoux while preventing the town from panicking as she tries to catch a killer who's turned "trick or treat" into the darkest diversion of all—murder.

Mistletoe is Murder: Bijoux Mystery Series Book 5

Skeletons with secrets, prohibition pirates, and holiday hijinks...

Morgan Hart is hoping for a boring Christmas. After eight months of murderous mayhem in her hometown of Bijoux, Michigan, she just wants to snuggle under a warm blanket in front of a cozy fire, with a good book, a hot chocolate (extra marshmallows of course), and Griselda purring beside her. She might even work up the nerve to ask Caleb Joseph over for dinner. Cal, the attractive owner of the Raven's Nest bookstore, has become a good friend since Morgan moved back home to take on the job of police captain.

A bestselling mystery author, Cal recently purchased the old Lawrence Mansion on the edge of town and plans to throw a big Christmas Eve bash. But Morgan's holiday plans—romantic and otherwise—go up in smoke when dark and shadowy secrets are revealed during the clean-up of the 19th century-built home. Can Morgan and Cal uncover the ghostly truth or are they destined for a disastrous deck-the-halls?

ORACLE DREAMS TRILOGY

Historical/Paranormal Time Travel Romance Series

Through the Mists of Time: Book One

London 1865…Valerie Sherwood Brooks has lived her entire life vicariously through books.

Due to a childhood accident, which left her with a permanent limp, Valerie has grown up under the watchful eye of her protective parents. When her banker father announces he's taking the family to Italy to look into an investment opportunity, Valerie is overjoyed at the prospect of leaving London for the excitement of exploring the ancient ruins of Pompeii.

But the romantic young woman who yearns for adventure is unprepared when an earthquake shatters their visit to the old city. Valerie is flung back in time to 79 A.D. where she's thrust into a world of intrigue and danger in the grand home of the darkly handsome, Christos Marcellus. As Valerie tries to keep her wits about her, she is torn between her growing and complicated feelings for Christos and the impending doom of the coming eruption of Vesuvius—knowing it will bring death and destruction.

Shadow Dreams: Book Two

In the village of Paran, in the peaceful plane of Keilah, lurks an evil bent on destruction.

Bethany M'Doro, a Healer and a Knower, possesses the unique ability to see into the past. Her gifts make her invaluable on Paran's archeological digs. The team's most recent discovery—charred bones and a wooden box with an ornate comb—sparks a vision of Eitel, an ancient cult known for stealing souls. Children's souls. A mysterious woman also appears in Bethany's vision, a woman named Elizabeth Jessup, who recently traveled through a portal from the Earth plane.

A widow, Bethany relies on her father to watch over her daughter Sarah, while she is on her expeditions. When Bethany returns home to Paran, her worst fear has come to pass. Sarah is missing along with several other children from the village.

Bethany realizes the resurrected cult of Eitel is responsible for abducting Sarah and the other young ones. And their leader is the traveler, Elizabeth Jessup. Bethany's visions lead her to the Earth plane, to Devil's Gate, Nevada in 1875, to enlist the help of Connor Jessup—Elizabeth's husband—a broken and embittered man.

Bethany now faces the greatest challenges of her life—heal Connor and convince him to travel back with her to Paran to unravel the secrets of Eitel and save Sarah and the other children.

Pagan Fire: Book Three

In the ancient village of Tintagel, Cornwall when old magic still illuminates the night sky, a young warrior embarks on a quest to reclaim his rightful place and the woman who haunts his dreams…

Dylan mac Connall survived the slaughter of his family ten years ago by a traitor to their clan. A young boy at the time, he was rescued by Kate, a wise witch woman who taught him the ways of magic and warned him of the peril that lays ahead if he chooses a path of revenge.

Raised in an abbey by the Sisters of Saint Columba, Maere cu Llwyr is ready to take her full vows and become a nun. But when a handsome warrior named Dylan arrives and claims to be her rightful betrothed, Maere is shocked and afraid of what her future will bring. A wee child when she was abducted from her village, Maere has blocked the memories of that horrific night. She has no recollection of the powerful ancient magic dormant inside her. Or of the childhood friend, who now stands before her, determined, to unlock both Maere's mind and her power.

As Maere and Dylan travel back to Tintagel, they must face the mercurial goddess Morrigu, dangerous Viking raiders, and the evil man who destroyed their families. Can Maere and Dylan survive the battles to come and find their way back home and to each other?

The Oracle Dreams Trilogy is also available as a Boxed Set at amazon.com.

NON-FICTION

Visit ReikiOne.com, PresenceandShadow.com, and / or SacredPriestess Journeys.com for more information.

Beginnings: ReikiOne First Degree Manual

This manual covers the basics of Reiki training and practice, including history, principles, hand positions, and treatment guidelines. Also included is a brief introduction to the chakras and using crystals with Reiki.

The Deeper Journey: ReikiOne Second Degree Manual

The ReikiOne Second Degree Manual includes the three symbols traditionally associated with this degree, explanations and their use, methods of distance healing, sending Reiki through time and space, combining symbols for greater effect, the chakra system, the human aura, and a suggested reading list.

Reiki Master: ReikiOne Third Degree Manual Part A by Teri Barnett, Reiki Master Teacher

This book contains the 4th symbol, its use for Reiki treatments, a discussion of what it means to be a Reiki Master, and how to use crystal grids with Reiki.

Reiki Master Teacher: ReikiOne Third Degree Manual Part B

The Master Teacher Manual contains all the information your students need for stepping into Reiki Master Teacher - A review of the 4th symbol (plus additional data on this symbol), the 5th symbol for attunements, attunement instructions (individual and group), methods and ethics of teaching, getting in touch with your inner teacher, marketing ideas, an extensive reading list, and much more.

The Reiki Teacher's Handbook

A composite of all the ReikiOne Manuals, the Reiki Teacher's Handbook takes your teaching a step further. This book provides you with all the tools you'll need to teach Reiki. Written from the experienced perspective of a master Teacher of the Usui Shiki Ryoho method, you'll find this book adapts easily to other forms of Reiki and can grow with you as you progress on your teaching path.

Made in United States
Troutdale, OR
12/29/2024